The Bodice Ripper

The Bodice Ripper

A NOVEL

BYRON REMPEL

ENFIELD
&WIZENTY

Copyright © 2017 Byron Rempel

Enfield & Wizenty
(an imprint of Great Plains Publications)
233 Garfield Street
Winnipeg, MB R3G 2M1
www.greatplains.mb.ca

All rights reserved. No part of this publication may be reproduced or transmitted in any form or in any means, or stored in a database and retrieval system, without the prior written permission of Great Plains Publications, or, in the case of photocopying or other reprographic copying, a license from Access Copyright (Canadian Copyright Licensing Agency), 1 Yonge Street, Suite 1900, Toronto, Ontario, Canada, M5E 1E5.

Great Plains Publications gratefully acknowledges the financial support provided for its publishing program by the Government of Canada through the Canada Book Fund; the Canada Council for the Arts; the Province of Manitoba through the Book Publishing Tax Credit and the Book Publisher Marketing Assistance Program; and the Manitoba Arts Council.

Design & Typography by Relish New Brand Experience
Printed in Canada by Friesens

Library and Archives Canada Cataloguing in Publication

Rempel, Byron, 1962-, author
    The bodice ripper / Byron Rempel.

Issued in print and electronic formats.
ISBN 978-1-927855-71-3 (softcover).—ISBN 978-1-927855-72-0 (EPUB).—ISBN 978-1-927855-73-7 (Kindle)

    I. Title.

PS8585.E614B63 2017   C813'.54   C2017-900626-6
                                                C2017-900627-4

	ENVIRONMENTAL BENEFITS STATEMENT			
	Great Plains Publications saved the following resources by printing the pages of this book on chlorine free paper made with 100% post-consumer waste.			
TREES	WATER	ENERGY	SOLID WASTE	GREENHOUSE GASES
6 FULLY GROWN	3,007 GALLONS	3 MILLION BTUs	201 POUNDS	554 POUNDS
	Environmental impact estimates were made using the Environmental Paper Network Paper Calculator 3.2. For more information visit www.papercalculator.org.			

Canadä

FSC
www.fsc.org
MIX
Paper from responsible sources
FSC® C016245

FOR GENEVIÈVE
who supports me in all circumstances
Here is the book we made, you and me
The life we made, that's another story

This is a work of fiction. Names, characters, businesses, places, events and incidents are either the products of the author's fantasies or wish fulfillment from repressed unconscious desires. Any resemblance to actual persons, living or dead, or actual events is purely coincidental, except for the Attila fellow. Certain universities and political entities are mentioned, but the characters and incidents that revolve around them are the product of my own daydreams. I respect and admire those who devote their lives trying to educate slow learners like myself. No bunny was harmed in the making of this novel.

Table of Contents

Part I: Ambiguous Groping	**11**
1. A Little Turbulence in 53A	13
2. Social Networking in the Early Middle Ages	33
3. Gothic Revival	46
4. Woman in Jeopardy	55
5. Special Operations	67
6. You Have Pomegranate Juice on Your Chin There	76
7. There Will Be Love	80
8. Stranded With A Stranger	98
9. Checkmate	112
Part II: Hot Bacon	**117**
10. The Risky Journey Bath	119
11. The Limit for Wounded Alpha Males	128
12. Are We History?	137
13. First Response	143
14. Anna Eden Elsewhere	153
15. Elopement Protocol (or, A Thousand Suns)	158
16. Sympathetic and Contagious Magic	165
17. Black Ice	177
18. Pleasures of the Flesh	180
Part III: Here Come the Sun King	**197**
19. Bunny	199
20. Harassment Assessment	206
21. Appropriate Risks	214
22. Ghastly, Unexpected Ends	220
23. The Queen of Coleridge Park	230

Part I:
Ambiguous Groping

> Happy love has no history.
> — Denis de Rougemont

1. A Little Turbulence in 53A

Professor Anna Hill uttered a vow on the first day of autumn, in the wake of her claimed thirty-ninth birthday, twenty-six weeks plus one day before she finally freed herself and a cat from certain doom. She vowed to live an exotic romance, and appeared that night at a costume party dressed as a medieval nun.

Enter the Moor, ibn Rushd, Averroes. He smelled of new wine, his accent (if not his moustache) dripped butter and cream. A weathered face jutted from a scarf that brooded on his head. Anna hoped the moustache was part of the costume, but it didn't matter when it came to providence. His real name was Christophe and his real work was of troubadours and their disappearance. "*Le crépuscule des troubadours.*" He had a little place on the Seine in Paris, where unlike Montreal it never snowed. The natives here, he inevitably said, had a word for each kind of snow.

The Inuit, Anna informed him, used recursively addable derivational suffixes, so there was only one base word for snow. Perhaps he was instead thinking of the many curses Montrealers threw at the stuff.

She had to stop with the wine at these faculty parties, where choral music was the preferred dance floor hit. Somewhere the Allegri *Miserere*, the Vatican's once secret incantation, curled like a rose vine above a stony chant. Her eyes closed and she saw herself and the French man Dr. Zhivago-ing through the kind of snow best suited for sleighs, shivered as she felt the ice palace, heard him whisper and shout her name.

Christophe backed away from the nun in front of him. Her closed eyes, lips parted, hands clasped at her breast. He was familiar with the varieties of religious experience, but had never been so close to their practice.

Pocahontas danced her way between them, unartfully clad in a few scraps of leather and a handful of feathers. She was not Status Indian, and had likely augmented other aspects of herself as well. Nevertheless, the talking points interested Christophe enough to divulge to Pocahontas that the week coming he would conduct a conference in Paris, and wouldn't it be agreeable to appreciate it together. *Challenges to Heteronormative Troubadours in Post-Intentional Phenomenology* the theme, how women were understood and misunderstood under attack, unpacked performativity inside the bedroom.

But Pocahontas, never impressed by schooling and at the party only by accident, had already retreated. Anna opened her eyes. In Paris, she breathed. Your Paris.

A man dressed as Jesus the carpenter appeared at the kitchen door, locked eyes with Anna. When she turned back, Christophe was gone.

Six days later on the way to check-in Anna waved away at least three proposals, one of which was rather handsome, to help her with her luggage. She kept at bay any impure thoughts as the security officer followed the contours of her body with his wand. She avoided a peek into the cockpit to assess the pilot. As she squeezed down the aisle towards 53A she was ready, as she had been the few other times she boarded planes, to sit beside a man of grace, elegance and charm.

She checked the boarding pass again, but had memorized her seat number days ago. She had also chosen her outfit, test-driven a few perfumes, and researched the fuel capacity of the Boeing 777-300ER. Only the man in the seat next to hers was not the right man: she was a woman. In a suit. The woman held a precarious tower of loose pages on her lap, and sighed as Anna jostled by.

Anna ignored the sigh. Little bothered Anna now. She had not refused when her mother handed her an ornate pillbox with four magic pills inside. She'd sliced them into quarters and at the gate swallowed the first collection of Clonazepam snacks. Now in her seat she took two more quarters so that (in her mother's poetic version) she'd already be in the clouds the moment the plane left earth. As she slipped on her camouflage-print sleep mask, the one that brought out the highlights in her red hair, she felt prescriptively calm for almost anything that flight could bring.

"That mask work for you, honey?"

The plane left the ground.

Anna drew up a corner of her mask. The air was grey outside the windows. Grey inside too. Her window wept. The plane never left the potholed clouds. She shut her eyes again. One good air bump got a few laughs from the boys in front of her. Anna knew that in her reality she traveled on a bus down an ill-maintained gravel road, a defrocked priest accompanying her to a cliffside *hacienda*. She let out a feigned snort that would match her insouciance on that bus.

Beside her, the businesswoman took the sound as an answer to her question.

"Couldn't do that. Feel too trapped."

Anna said nothing.

"'Specially with all this chop."

This was the thing with travel: the complete absence of control. You could prepare for weeks, organize and coordinate schedules, glean from blogs and guidebooks and knowledge of friends, and in the end be left with a handful of chaff. But Anna wouldn't let it affect her, because she was on her way to a spontaneous rendezvous, unlike anything she'd done before. Inside her mask Anna stared at the ceiling of her mind and wished it as featureless as a prairie sky. She inhaled deeply, one time. She folded her hands together, a saint in earshot of temptation. She would not lift the mask.

"Block things out," the woman said, "but it won't get you far. I should know. Tried it for years. Blocked out my therapist for fifty-two thousand eight hundred dollars of sessions. Which is what freed me up, you know: budget constraints. Husband said: go well, or go homeless. Which is some sports cliché. And then he went."

Normally, at home, Anna could correct papers while she watched television, talk to her mother on the phone while she scrubbed burned pots. In her classroom she uncovered Spanish priests and bishops in the throes of twelfth-century celibacy while the insistent siren of a snowplow outside the window seduced three hundred and forty-three restless freshmen. But this—this stentorian voice that chipped away at the foundation of Anna's synaptic peace—it brought everything to the verge of collapse. But she had the solution: Paris still needed a plan.

The conference, for one.

At that moment one of Anna's shoes hid beneath the seat. The potholes on the way up through the clouds sent it out of reach. She jiggled the other shoe from her toe. She felt her pulse, and breathed a few deep inhales.

The most appropriate place to dazzle Christophe, multiple choice:

>   a) In the Sorbonne's *Grand amphithéâtre*, with its statues of Descartes and Pascal and Richelieu under the golden domes, where, during an otherwise interminable debate among international historians, she stands up in the balcony and with one profound but surprisingly simple conclusion, obliterates all other research and opinion, and the scholars are left babbling about Christophe's fortune to be with this intellectual Amazon;
>
>   b) During a tour of a *château* half-submerged in a river, when he, without warning, presses her against a wall that clicks open to reveal a secret and close stairway, and as the tour guide's voice echoes away, Christophe leads her through that murky passage into the sun-drenched boudoir of a king's mistress, and slides a massive bolt to lock the door as she resists only long enough to let her gaze take in the erotic tapestries and candelabras and a four-poster bed of astounding proportions;
>
>   c) On a hidden street deep in the history of the city on a café terrace, over *cafés crèmes*, as everything else fades away and it's the two of them, in *their* Paris, illuminating embodied qualities of gender. Hands brush when they reach for the sugar substitute at the same time. Their eyes flash to each other's faces. A shock of recognition mutates into passion. A tourist couple walks by, marvels at their perfect tableau of love, envy in their voices… "And such gorgeous shoes," the woman says…

"You're not asleep, are you?"

Anna said nothing, but didn't jiggle her shoe.

"The way you fidget. Maybe you should have a glass of wine."

Anna sighed. Her hand rose from beneath the flimsy blanket. She lifted a corner of her mask.

"Peek-a-boo," the woman said. She held two small bottles of red wine. "We *are* headed for France." She folded down Anna's tray and placed a plastic glass and one of the bottles in front of her. She'd already twisted them open. *"Bon voyage."*

Anna brought the mask up to her forehead and sprouted corkscrews of red hair. She was glad her seatmate wasn't a man after all.

"You know how I could tell you weren't asleep? Your fingers were rigid on the armrest. Look at the dents you left."

Anna looked, but there were none.

Had the woman given her name? Anna recognized the dream quality of the Clonazepam her mother said she might feel. So little to worry about in the world. When you thought about it. Or didn't.

It was now black outside her tiny window. Anna tried to worry. Was it early morning? Late evening? The video screen in front of her showed a map. Ocean predominated. The screen claimed they were thirty-six thousand feet in the air, and boasted of five hundred and fifty-three miles an hour. She tried to worry: there was only cold above and beneath her. And then Anna smiled, and watched her hand swim towards the tray table and the plastic glass of wine.

"Atta girl," the woman said.

They clinked glasses, a dull bump. The wine smelled foreign on the plane.

"You'll stay in Paris?"

Paris. The word brought her closer to consciousness. She was on her way to Paris.

"Yes."

"Me too."

Anna nodded. Christophe would be there. She may stay in Paris the rest of her life.

"I may stay there the rest of my life."

The woman raised her eyebrows. "First time, huh?"

Anna's head bobbed.

The hostesses came by with plastic trays of plastic food.

"My name's Julia," said her seatmate. Julia waited a few beats. "You?"

"Oh. Professor Anna Hill." Anna could not explain why she had called herself *Professor*.

"A prof," Julia said, as if academics were a rare sight thirty thousand feet above the Atlantic. "Let me guess: Literature."

"Medieval history."

"Whew. Close one. So, Professor Anna Hill: you going to teach in Paris?"

"Oh no. A conference."

"What on?"

Julia left her tray of food sealed, and instead stopped the hostess. "A couple more bottles of the house red," she said.

"The Siege on the Castle of Love," Anna said while she tore apart the sandwich wrap with her teeth.

"Huh."

"An interdisciplinary conference on the religion, culture, work, cuisine and ceremony of a castle under siege."

"Wow," said Julia, "a real potboiler."

The woman spoke like she'd come out of the 1940s. But she wasn't much older than Anna. She let her grey hair show, in a girlish ponytail.

"These things lasted years, you know," Anna said.

"The conferences?"

Anna turned to look at Julia, but her eyes closed as she sipped wine.

"I need to research a paper. The culture part. *Re-Gendering Liminal Exoticization.*"

"You've all got such cute titles."

"It's where historians get to kick out the jams."

"I'll say. I bet things get crazy at these conferences."

"Absolutely historical," Anna said.

Anna knew the conference would be Medieval Studies as she'd always known it. Tribal pow-wows she'd joined before. New theories, the same biases. The one-upmanship of knowledge: three hundred scholars, one hundred and fifty papers, a shipment of rubber chickens as bad as the airline's. Except not. This time it was the Latin Quarter, the Sorbonne. This time it was Paris. The chickens would not be rubbery: they would be exquisite, bathed in butter and cream, tended by hands that nightly plucked mushrooms from hidden woods, that freed the chicks to play in fields of wild rosemary bushes and thyme and… and… there was another herb, what was it? Whatever. The invitation was official: this time it was Paris, and this time it came from an urbane and wealthy Frenchman who probably had a *garçonnière* that hung over the Seine. One of those cute little European convertibles too, steered with those kid leather gloves he sported, to whisk her away from the drones of the conference and on to his own vineyard, where at the ancestral manse they would be welcomed by three inquisitive wolfhounds and an ancient but kindly caretaker named Gustave. That was the thing with travel: the world was open and infinite.

Fifteen minutes after the turbulence Anna still giggled, even though the shirt she'd chosen in which to greet Christophe (an off-white blouse with festive sleeves and collar) was now spotted with pink

Rorschach tests. From her breast rose the musty smell of rustic French villages at the end of a September's day.

"You're all right, though?" Julia asked.

"My paper," Anna continued, a new wine glass in hand, "was called *Lie Still and Think of Spain: Homosocially Segregated Environments among Early Visigoth Settlers in Iberia, 450-600 AD.*"

Julia gazed into the empty video screen. Now every time the plane bumped, she grabbed the armrest. "Sounds like a ringer. You got some mayo there. On your chin."

"My book, though. Maybe you've heard of it? It's called *Love in the Material-Semiotic Realm: Gender, Death, and Medieval Courtship.* But you know what?"

Anna was in a confessional mood. She wasn't sure, was Clonazepam the truth drug? Or was that Champagne?

"The book had nothing to do with love. In the courts, daughters and sons were exchanged for political maneuvers. So little source material exists on the commoners. And because of that it was cold, and hard, and footnoted to death."

"The love?"

"It sold two hundred and thirty-eight copies."

"Well then."

Anna put her hand over her mouth. All this talk made her too open to the world. Now, she wouldn't say any more until asked.

"Did you…" the woman started.

"It sold well because the cover had a graphic fourteenth-century woodcut that featured fellatio."

Julia stopped drinking long enough to look at Anna. A man across the aisle was attentive too.

"The first reviewer called the book a 'Huge achievement.' There was a promise of more illustrations inside."

The man cleared his throat, and Julia collapsed in laughter on Anna's shoulder. They spilled wine over each other and pointed at the man with his face now buried in a magazine. They were schoolgirls. They were drunk. They didn't care.

The hostesses brought more wine, although Anna waved away Julia's hand. Julia ignored her. Somewhere over the white darkness of Greenland, Anna rallied to use the toilet again. She looked over the seats from the rear of the plane, tried to focus her eyes. Every woman's video screen was tuned to the same romantic comedy. As one they all threw back their heads in laughter at the kooky heroine's antics, then sniffed and wiped tears away with choreographed precision. When her eyes focused most screens showed only the interminable progress of the plane across the Atlantic.

"I'm on my way to meet a French man and fall in love," Anna confessed to Julia while she searched for her seatbelt.

"Anyone, or a particular one you got in mind?"

"Oh, particular."

"How lovely for you," Julia said. "I fell out of love and I'm on my way to divorce a French man."

"Oh no," said Anna.

"No sympathy, please. Should've known."

"Known what?"

"Not to marry a playwright."

"I didn't know."

"See? I tell my clients: CEO, rancher, spy, policeman, fighter pilot." Julia enumerated as she held up five fingers. The ring was still on the fourth finger, but the stone had fallen out.

"Your clients?" Anna asked.

"Worst is, you see yourself on stage later. If you go to the theatre. I don't. That's the only good thing. Hardly anybody does."

Julia stared straight into the screen in front of her and touched the ring on her finger.

"And your Frenchman?" Julia said, not able to bear self-pity and silence for longer than fifteen seconds. "What's he do?"

"Um," Anna said. "He's a professor too."

"Yikes. Not your boss?"

"No no."

"You're not pregnant?"

"Not in the least."

"Suffer from amnesia spells?"

"Not that I recall."

The woman seemed relieved. "Don't mean to pry," she said. "A little quiz I give."

"So you're a teacher too?"

"Could say that. I wouldn't. More of a babysitter."

"Can I pry?"

"You Canadians, so polite. Where I come from we call it conversation. Fire away."

"You're American?" It was a surprise to no one.

"Philly. Had a little meeting in Montreal. Can you say 'out and about' for me?"

"Out and about?"

"That's cute. The accent's not as punchy as some parts of your country though. I always got my French husband to say 'The thing.' Tray sexy. 'Ze sing.' Try it sometime on your man. Make sure there's a bedroom nearby."

Anna chortled, blushed, looked up at the plastic ceiling. "So let me guess," she said, her hand on Julia's arm, "a dating agency for lonely rich women? And your clients chase spies and cowboys?"

"They'd better. Or we drop them."

"That is so so dreamy. The spies I mean. And it all works out in the end?"

"I hope so. Or *I'd* be dropped."

"It isn't your dating agency?"

"It ain't no dating agency, honey. I'm an editor with Harlequin Romance."

Anna let out a bark. She wasn't sure if Julia knew it was a laugh, so she coughed a bit, then interspersed it with a few more barks, then drank some wine out of the flimsy plastic cup too quickly and began to cough for real.

"Sorry," she said. "Your clients. They're authors."

"Thank you. I'm sorry too."

"No, I meant. A Canadian thing. We're sorry. We apologize." Anna reached for her cup of wine again. The stuff parched her mouth.

"We accept. People have ideas about romance novels, you know. Even women. And especially *professors*."

"Oh," Anna said, only it came out as more of a squeak than she had intended, "not me. Not me." She'd written a quickie paper on supermarket romances when she was an undergrad. Couldn't miss with a feminist target the size of a loading dock. Something about passive women and an insistence on sexual violence. She straightened out her ruffled blouse, pulled back her hair. "Then that pile of paper, that was someone's potential novel?"

"No. That was someone's potential divorce."

"Oh. Right. But you know what's too funny? I research romance too."

Julia didn't look convinced.

"Well see *romance*, you know… it doesn't mean love."

"Damn straight."

"Well no. Romance was a heroic narrative. *Medieval*. Like the King Arthur stories. Magic and adventures, no need for princesses in towers. Told or sung in the languages that stemmed from the Romans, so they began to be called *Romances*. The Birth of Romance. You see?"

"Okay Professor. So you write poems about knights in buffed armour."

"I never write poetry. Poetry is self-indulgent and tasteless. Like gruel."

"Gruel is self-indulgent?"

"Yes. It wants everything to be gruel."

Anna wanted to be witty, but it so rarely worked. "I don't write. I mean, not that way. And then you can't confuse it with Romanticism, the intellectual movement. You know: Blake and Coleridge, Byron and the Shelleys."

"Attorneys at law."

"I always tell my students, 'Listen to Chopin and read *Frankenstein* under a canvas by Turner. That's Romanticism."

"Or overkill. But you wrote a new book?"

"It's a collapse," Anna began on autopilot, until the soft pop of the cabin bell sounded, enough to let the pills in and fade her voice and it took her a few seconds to remember, "a re-construct of interrupted gender correctives," until another pilot's mumbled version of chatter came over the tin speaker, the oral equivalent of a doctor's written prescription: authoritative, indecipherable, prone to understatement. The pilot didn't advise the passengers about turbulence, but instead narrated the antics of a heroine on the seatback screens, currently embarrassed at a party. And then the voice became her father, kind but unequivocal about her seatbelt. Told her she was too deep into the details again, and couldn't see the sky for the clouds. In front of Anna the little plane on her screen loop-de-looped over the North Atlantic Ridge.

※※※

"Wait a minute," Julia said while she poured them another glass, "you mean you'd make the hero of your romance novel a *poet?*"

"Nineteen shentury," said Anna. "Century. I wish I could read poetry."

"Oh that'll sell. The lovers die of consumption, do they?"

"I haven't outlined it that far."

"Not far at all. You got a year to spare? You know that mystery writer Dorothy Sayers?"

"I don't think she…"

"It looks simple, she said, but so do some little frocks. Not the kind of thing any fool can run up in half an hour with a machine. Listen, I'll give you one word that'll save you a bunch of trouble: Damaged Alpha Male."

"Three words."

"Wanted to make sure you're awake. Ya see? Strong. Irresistible. Poets are not strong. Poets are resistible."

"Not what you'd expect from an editor."

"*Au contraire.*" She spoke French with an accent flat as the Great Plains. "Honey: the guy I want to divorce wrote poetry. I know of what I speak. All wonderful till they have to *do* something."

"At the start, he's alone among the cliffs and heather, calls her name…" Anna saw Christophe peer through his tousled hair into the distance, look for her ship, her plane. Torn apart by this prolonged absence, but keeping it all inside. Whatever century it is. As he walks towards the cliffs something tugs on his long-tailed coat, and he turns to pull it from the rose-bush thorns, but he's caught, he's trapped, he needs to be rescued by her but where is she? He kicks at the bush with his riding boots, now scarred and saddened. His perfect exterior comes apart, his ascot, askew, takes wing with the wind, flies towards the white cliffs and he watches it leap off the lip, nothing he can do, where *is* she? He pulls at his coat and it comes free, but not before a thousand rose petals are loosed in the wind and their scent whirlwinds around him with the memory of…

"My favorite place for poets," said Julia, "on a cliff. Often they jump. Or if we're all lucky there'll be a good stiff wind."

Anna was still in the heather, eyes half-closed. How did one tie an ascot? Maybe he had a scarf, tossed about his neck. That would have to be looked up. And were there roses among heather, and heather among cliffs, and where were these cliffs? And when was then? She'd have an advantage at this, that was sure. Research, and documents, and footnotes. Although editors like Julia couldn't allow footnotes in historical romances. But they should. She could begin a trend.

"You're at a disadvantage, you know. A history prof. You'll use footnotes like little tortures, then bury your readers alive with boredom."

"But historical romance," Anna said. "Love and history, I've got it covered."

"You've got to keep it on a leash. The strong hero, and your ten plots. *Marriage of Convenience*."

"I've never even dated for convenience," said Anna. "Unless you count the history department chair from Rostov-on-Don. Dmitri. The date at his convenience."

He'd wandered the halls, asked after a tie he'd lost. Dmitri Bushnov was so pitiable when she found it (in his office) that she accepted dinner at a Chinese restaurant. He had tried to kiss her but she couldn't do it, not after he'd ordered litchis in syrup. He already had a permanent aroma of pepper vodka about him. But he was still in her camp at the University.

"Two: *Stranded with a Stranger.*"

Another reason she avoided travel whenever possible. Friends turned out to be strangers.

"Then, *Runaway Bride, Secret Baby, Reunion Romance*…"

There had been so many dates. So little romance. The reunion—she'd tried to hook up with that whitewater raft guide in Maine, the one who'd rescued her. So what if it had been a twelve-year-old kid who'd pulled her out of the rapids, the guide had supervised. She'd tried to rekindle that campfire for a good six years now.

"…*Back From the Dead, Mistaken Identity*…"

Deadbeats, mistakes about identity. As Julia ticked off titles on both hands, Anna looked out the window into the stars where some glimmer of sunrise wished itself on the curved horizon. The editor enumerated her plots, but by now Anna only heard a rosary of romantic *Hail Marys*. The woman counted off the catastrophes and fiascos of Anna's life. Please stop, Anna said, although she wasn't sure if she said it out loud. The plane's drone blended with Julia's list.

"…and of course, *Woman in Jeopardy*, without whom we'd all be lost, and *The Dad Next Door*. That's nine."

It seemed like Julia had called up all of Anna's delinquent dates, because the line-up in front of the airplane bathroom was all men, and included The Dad Next Door with what looked like a Secret Baby in his arms. She blinked, wished them away. One by one they disappeared through the tiny door. They left an empty space. The definition of her love life. Her head rested against the cold of the plastic window, and beads of moisture gathered there, and ran into her eyes.

"Ten, though: ten is a collective, a grab bag. They're my favourites. So: *Boss-Secretary*; *Amnesia*; *Virgin Heroine* (as if); *Pregnant Heroine* (more like it); *On the Run*; and our winner ladies and gentlewomen…"

Julia's voice echoed through Anna's head with the hum of the plane.

"…*The Rancher and the City Girl*. That's it. Love is all about tension, you know. Can't miss. That, and happily ever after. Not too much to ask?"

When Julia did turn to Anna, she only saw Anna's shoulders shaking, and the blanket up to her face, and heard the unmistakable melody of a woman sobbing, for her life.

There were moments on the six-hour flight when Julia didn't speak, didn't try to fill emptiness with chatter, with professional revelations about her romance, with acid-dipped memories of her French ex, and this moment, however brief, was one of those. For almost fifty-six seconds she waited for the tears of Anna to ebb.

"Oh look," Julia said, "I think we're over England."

The sky glowed brighter beyond the channel.

"Jane Austen and all that," Julia said in an execrable English accent.

England for Anna only meant Paris was that much closer. If Paris was closer, so was her rendezvous with Christophe, although now she couldn't recall how they had agreed to meet, or where, or, come to think of it, that mysterious scamp, if he had even said he'd meet her at the airport, although it couldn't have been otherwise. That was the thing about travel. You can stay up all night atop the ocean, float on medication and cheap red wine, smell of a vineyard, your eyes with their own luggage, and then someone mentions *Woman in Jeopardy* and you see your empty shell for what it is, no tissues in sight. That's why one didn't travel.

Over the channel in a panic over today, Anna escaped again to yesterday. Above the beaches of Normandy she became her father, searched for emergency landings by moonlight. And it seemed clear to her that the romantic fault line lay with her father. For taking off like that. The idea seemed clear until the gravity of the past pulled the plane down, and the sky lightened. This was a new day. Things would be different in Paris. Everything. If she could find her other shoe. She'd need that shoe. In Paris. She could buy some. Shoes.

Anna succumbed to fatigue in that so-desired Elysian Field, and the side of her head stuck to the plastic window. The camouflage sleep mask caught in the tangle of her hair to create a loopy top-knot. Her eyes were kohled from tears. She immediately dreamed of French cathedral bells. She could not tell if they were for a wedding or funeral.

The bells tolled and softly popped.

And through it all, a voice rose, sometimes of her father, or the priest, from this day forward, to have and to hold, "…Paris out the left window," the pilot said over the speakers. The plane made an abrupt shift toward earth, and Anna's ears popped open. Morning came to France. Anna saw the plane's interior pulsate with a virginal glow, as if she and all the other passengers had drawn out expectations from the City of Light, and faith and dreams haloed their heads, hope burst from their breasts, a Medieval manuscript of *très riches heures* come to life. She squinted out the window into the golden haze below in a search for the twin towers of Notre Dame.

"Good morning," Julia said cheerily. "You were out for a good fifteen minutes. Isn't it awful?"

"Paris?"

"The air. Pollution makes it yellow. Glows like Chernobyl."

Anna stepped into Charles de Gaulle airport and began to

cough. She had persevered until then, had maneuvered down the plane aisle and into the airport with only one high-heeled shoe. The other had disappeared, another of her father's magic tricks. Repeated inquiries and a search by the aircrew had done nothing to bring it back. And by the time she was off the plane, the only help Anna had from Julia was a crumpled business card in her palm, which when smoothed out revealed a diamond as its logo. She remembered a "goodbye" somewhere, although it seemed Julia had stepped off the airplane in midflight, and trusted her own wings to take her away.

At the luggage carousel Anna hauled off the first of her two suitcases, the smaller vintage one, with no gallant offers of help. She would have refused anyway. She had to open the suitcase right there to get a pair of shoes, and would not want strange men to catch sight of any flimsy underwear, or what she believed was an even flimsier research paper. But there were no shoes in that suitcase, they were all in the one that still hadn't appeared. Anna stood up from her search. The airport swayed and pixilated around the edges. She checked her watch, which for some reason was now faceless. The *vin d'honneur* for the opening session of the conference was this "afternoon" at the Sorbonne, that much she remembered. She wondered if her fingers would make air quotes around "afternoon" when she told Christophe this story. She wondered if the French used air quotes. Anna steadied herself on a luggage cart. She would have to close her eyes in the hotel room for a while. She would have to. She would.

She didn't have to wait that long. As she watched the slow motion arrival of her second suitcase Anna lunged toward it in stuttered phases. The bag proved to be made of lead, and magnetic, so that her arm followed the suitcase, and her body thereafter, until she found herself on a carousel of horses in a medieval fair, like the merry-go-round she wanted to see at the base of the *Sacre Cœur*, while she fluttered her hand at her loyal subjects on the sides. Her fingers came up to her forehead to sweep away what she believed was stray hair, and then the other passengers watched her one shoe dangle on her heel, until she disappeared through the rubber curtains.

2. Social Networking in the Early Middle Ages

"This is you," the man said. He held the book in his hands like a weapon.

In a room with fogged windows Anna's pills wore down. She forgot how she got into this room, or why. A French man with suspect motives. He took her pillbox and its discontents. He struggled to open it but could not.

At her elbow, four copies of *Love Gets Medieval: Torture as Processual Language*. The back cover called her "a meticulous scholar, with a rebel's heart."

Why hadn't Christophe come to get her at the airport? Anna had only one question, but the unsmiling man in front of her echoed questions. What is the destination? How long do you stay? What do you carry besides these pills? She heard them as Zen koans. She breathed in, held it, exhaled. The agent didn't want practical answers. He wanted her to look within. Did she hide contraband? What kind of rebel was she? What is the sound of one heart beating?

Anna understood it was no time for meditation. Righteous indignation was more appropriate. Romance heroines, for example, would not tolerate this mistreatment. They would not meditate on riddles, but combat the tormentor with feisty quips. Anna had so far left Christophe thirteen texts and three phone messages. None of them were clever.

If Christophe had been at the airport how different everything would be. He would understand this man's accent, a strange southern French lilt. *He* wouldn't ask the agent over and over what he was trying to say, or demand where he was born. He would have held her arm at the baggage carousel so she wouldn't have gone for a ride in the first place. He would have stormed in here, a mistral of vengeance. But until he answered her messages Anna preened in that room, checked her makeup on her phone until the agent thought she took pictures and confiscated that too.

Back home, back at university, the faculty believed she lived a secret and tumultuous life. Now she almost believed it. She would have anecdotes. We professors are like cats! she would say. We answer to no one.

Her tormentor saw before him a kitten with her eyes still shut. He had seen many things in his brief career, and hearing a drugged professor plead with him about an academic conference was not going to weaken his resolve. When Anna lied that she was supposed to lead a roundtable on the Impasse Between Material and Symbolic Medieval Torture that afternoon he maintained an uninterested visage. Only last week he had dug out a highly personal collection from a suitcase of a man interested in the same area of study.

He asked Anna, Where were you going truly? You turn and turn. And every time you pass the baggage men they put themselves on their knees in front of you with devotion, and will not touch you, a battered saint in a vision of loops. Something like that. Anna wasn't sure about her simultaneous translation.

"I'm in love with a Frenchman," she tried finally. "We have to meet."

Did the agent's face melt a degree? He looked directly at her, put down the book. Placed a hand on either side of her chair. "What you have done is very serious. We must return you *chez vous*. To Montreal. Do you have a husband waiting back home?"

"I just said, I'm in love with a Frenchman."

He raised his eyes. "Yes, but there is a husband?"

They were back in Zen territory again.

"If I ever get out of here there will be. And if I don't, it'll be your fault I end up sad and alone in some pathetic home for wayward singles." It was the best she could do for witty repartee, and it had no noticeable effect on the agent.

"We check on the next plane to Montreal this afternoon. You return. We keep the pills."

The agent was long and lean, his uniform sharp at the edges. His eyes were committed to her. He smelled of nutmeg. Anna was sure that she smelled like fear. Her clothes were rumpled and her eyes blurry.

"You have nothing to fear."

He hadn't said that. She made him say it. The fault of the room, with its limited oxygen. The more she saw how serious her confinement was, how unlikely it was that she would see Christophe or even Paris outside of this airport, the more she surrendered to an edited scenario. The agent would ask questions, and she would answer. They would communicate. He would ask, Do you trust me?

Of course not, she would say.

You have nothing to fear. Unless you hide something.

I'm not, she would say. I don't trust you.

He touched her shoulder and her body shivered. His grip tightened. But you should trust me. I only...

Through the tips of his fingers she felt his desire. He could do nothing to hide it. She heard his breathing behind her, heavier now.

Wait, she says. I'll tell you everything.

He is in front of her now, holding her wrists. Her hands tremble. In one fluid motion he lifts her from the chair and presses her against the wall. The brick is cold on her back, and his breath hot on her neck.

What are you hiding? he asks. His hand clutches at her blouse, reaches underneath. His other hand glides between her legs, searching. She struggles against him, but she only feels him hard.

I can't return, she says. I'll die if you send me back there. She tries to touch his face but he pulls her hand away. Don't make me, she says, and her lips part as his eyes narrow on hers.

Another agent stuck his head through the opened door. "There's a noon flight to Montreal."

Anna was back in the chair, the agent behind a table, his hand on her book. "You are not thirty-nine," he said. "Not according to your passport."

Anna shook her head. More to clear her thoughts than disagree.

"No one told you lying is the worst thing you can do here?"

"It's not lies," she said. "It's words. And let me tell you everything. I'm not a professor. Only an assistant. My real work is... I'm a romance novelist. *Les romans à l'eau de rose*. I use a pen name. I'm on my way to a meeting with my editor. Julie. Julia."

The agent's eyes were forceful, and dark, and maybe they narrowed. She wasn't sure how eyes did that. "What are your other titles," he asked.

"*Under the Spell of Provence*," she said. "*Woman in Jeopardy. The Playboy Sheikh's Virgin Stable-Girl. The End of the Affair. Secret Dad. The Rancher and the City Girl. Random Acts of Complicated Kindness. Lives of Girls and Women.*"

"Wait," he said. He stepped out of the room. Anna knew she'd gone too far. That she'd just screwed her chances of making Christophe fall in love with her in the most romantic city in the world. She began to pack her books.

The agent came back in the room, carrying a small leather bag. He set it down in front of her, unzipped it, and pulled out a book. He placed it in front of her. *Le sheikh charmeur et la palfrenière ingénue. The Playboy Sheikh's Virgin Stable-Girl.*

"My favourite book," said the agent. He let his icy face allow the crack of a smile. "I have read it three times. Me and my boyfriend read it to each other before bed. You will sign it?"

Anna grabbed his pen, began signing her real name, then stopped quick enough to scribble the name on the cover with a flourish and a throbbing heart.

"I'm flattered," she said, and she was, she would begin to cry soon.

The agent picked up the book and held it to his chest. "You may go now." *N'importe quoi*, he thought. He'd been ready to let her go anyway. Another delusional academic.

She touched his hand. Her lies tasted of sugar and vanilla and magic, and within minutes she walked free from the airport and ready for Christophe's arms.

This was the Right Bank, the wrong bank. The conference was across the river in the Latin Quarter, with Voltaire and Hugo as neighbours, Baudelaire down the street and his bleeding pen. That university. The one established in the Middle Ages and the model for every after.

Anna paced in her cell. She'd been happy to find a cheap hotel room, but it had three single beds and no room to move. She'd completely missed the *vin d'honneur*, but Christophe's presentation was scheduled in the next hour at the conference. All she wanted to do was collapse on the bed. But the sheets and blankets were relics, so she worried between the bed and a desk and a chair, and missed only a cross and string of beads.

She took a cab and got out in front of the Notre-Dame, would walk the few blocks to the university. Her fingers were cold. When she walked by a steaming stand on the sidewalk it blew warmth and a smell that she would forever associate with Paris. A man made crepes in sweeping motions, folded them in triangles, slipped them in their pyjamas. She ordered one with Nutella. When Anna bit into it the chocolate erupted and flowed onto her fingers. On the Petit Pont she licked them, in full view of the tourists and bridges and history. She never wanted to leave. There was only one element missing, and he was probably already in the small conference room, clearing his throat and peering over his glasses. Searching for her.

He would be surprised to see her, thrilled by her spontaneity, her impetuous nature. Her kooky way of dressing. But then not—he would say he knew all along she would come, and they would run out onto the boulevards and terraces…well not run onto the boulevards, that would be crazy with this traffic, even for a woman like herself. And not *running* through the terraces like a couple of stray dogs with stolen slices of *jambon*, but lounging, delighting in the warming sun. And that crepe on the bridge. Her fingers. Sweet, and burning, and wet.

It was warm standing on the bridge. The afternoon sun. She hurried to the Sorbonne. To miss his talk would be unforgivable, and then how would she claim her expenses? In her thirty-ninth year, how could she forgive herself that she had never found and exploited love?

⚯

Christophe walked to the *Grand amphithéâtre*, his chin up but seeing nothing in front of him. The organizers had changed his venue, probably due to his popularity. But with the last-minute move he'd lose some audience.

He saw nothing, but had a good idea of what happened around him. Peripheral vision was the trick. Students kept to the side. Professors with their heads up—and so many of them studied their own footwear instead of their theories—should expect an imperceptible nod. Evaluation of rank was paramount at conferences, and those with unrecognizable name tags needn't be bothered with. Social refinement was absent among so many of them, especially the Americans, or the Germans, or really any academician outside of France. Those outside of Paris were also suspect. In fact, if he had to get specific about it, the only person who knew what he was doing, and how to do it, and why, was the esteemed professor separating the masses in the hallway now.

He did agree with most of the professors however, that reading books and analyzing numbers were much more enjoyable than talking to people. The last time he was in an elevator he'd learned the man's complete life history, with digressions into Franco-American relations, in six floors. He had flinched when he first heard the way they'd renamed the conference: Social Networking in the Early Middle Ages.

Beside the door to the amphitheatre, an enterprising medievalist had set up a table advertising the construction of a brand-new thirteenth-century castle. With its promised "living archaeology" and scheduled visiting hours for tourists, Christophe immediately dismissed it, and the nerdy scholar behind the table, as an unwelcome invasion by Disney. He told the man as much, and sent him packing. He would not sully the doors of his event with spectacle.

※

Professor Anna Hill pinned a badge to her navy jacket. "Visiting Guest" it read, which was better than having no badge at all. At least it slowed some of the professors enough to read it as they hurried by. But she didn't get eye contact. This was the extent of her social networking, and this was early middle age.

Somewhere—she still hadn't found the room—Christophe was one of the few men who claimed his presentation would focus entirely on women, through his views on the troubadours' poems of love. The description said his exploration would include, but by no means be limited to, the existence, performance and sustainability of diverse scholarly, intellectual and material assemblages and topographies re the liminalities of gender and love.

That was clear enough. But whatever he talked about, she knew he wouldn't be like the rest of these academic troubadours. Like medieval singers, like much of the pop music she'd heard, all those precious words purported to be about glorious Woman and Love. But they were really about the writer, about what a deft weaver of words was the man. And Woman, the great subject, was only the means to the end of showing off their linguistic and academic power. The respected voices here were predominantly masculine.

The women's voices were muffled. But Christophe was different, and that's what made him an academic superstar.

That's why it was surprising to find, after she creaked open the conference room door, that the seats and the podium up front were empty. She was late, but not that late. She checked the door name and number, but that wasn't the problem either. Anna sat down on a chair. In a few minutes she got up again and asked people walking by if they knew of the lecture, until finally someone took pity on her, a lost and visiting guest.

By the time she arrived at the right room and saw Christophe behind his pulpit, the whole of the room cheered at some clever twist of words he employed, and he was already past his conclusion and into discussion.

"The only thing we know for sure," he said, and Anna felt his voice amplified by the speakers and echoing through her body, "is that there were no Women in those ages." The room filled with mumbles and small outcries. Anna smirked. She knew these methods, seeking out scandal and provocation to be remembered. "No women, at least not as we understand them, today. If we can even say that." More guffaws and masculine recognition. "Since the only thing we have to interpret them, the only primary source, is silence."

Anna recognized this as nothing new, nothing truly scandalous, since whole other conferences and tomes were built around the absence of women in history. The educated men who'd written all the sources had been whisked away from the company of women at an early age in court. They were left nostalgic and fascinated by those rare creatures. And they feared them too, feared the unseen, their subliminal powers.

"And if there was no such thing as Woman in the Middle Ages, then today there is no such thing as Gender. It is ever shifting through geography, culture, social contracts, through space and imagined spaces."

Maybe it wasn't his most inspired talk, Anna thought. She'd only seen the question and answers too, which weren't prepared. But she hadn't come here to be seduced by logic. They had a date, on a bridge. She took her time getting to the front of the room, waited while his devotees and partisans wore him down with praise, or his French peers argued and jockeyed for position. Christophe was coy with her. He glanced up sometimes, scanned the room. She kept her eyes dark and her lips moist. Finally a space opened and she stood in front of him. He plowed a hand through his hair.

"Well well," Anna said, "Enter the Moor."

"Pardon?"

"The Moor," Anna said. "At the costume party." She watched him think, scan her visitors name tag, then extend his hand as he looked to the door.

"Glad you enjoyed the lecture," he said in English, and shook her hand.

"I was the nun," Anna said. "*Unpacking Performativity in the Bedroom?*"

"Congratulations."

The impression wasn't the one she'd counted on. More groupie than Amazon. He turned and left the room. She didn't have his phone number or the place he was staying. She had nothing, nothing but the death of romance.

Anna's phone rang as she lay on one of her beds. But it was Julia from the plane. She invited Anna to an evening at what she called secret Paris, and Anna didn't even make a pretense of being busy or having to check an agenda. She couldn't find another taxi so kept walking. And when she got to the address behind the Palais-Royal and K-Mart Kafeteria she found a bistro and there was Julia and two of her romance novelists, tipsy already, and eager to sympathize with Anna's inability to connect with her man.

"They're scared," Julia said. "Sometimes you have to talk down to men. What our resident webgirl calls Compatibility Mode. You can have it turned on or off. Depends on how much you share."

The bistro was sweltering and gilded and potted with palms, a cathedral to French soul food: steak tartare, *foie gras*, *escargots*, rabbit, pig's feet, *crême brulée*. The hideout wasn't a secret to anybody, not Parisians nor tourists, though the Americans were kept to the noisy section. Anna hadn't eaten for twenty-three hours and it didn't look like the place to start.

"I don't have a webgirl. I have a TA girl."

"Compatible?"

"Organized. She insisted I wear heels but I lost one. She's all intentions."

"The road to hell is paved with cobblestones."

"Her idea of a romantic escape I guess. Like people who buy your little fantasies."

"A Harlequin bought every four seconds. Half of all paperbacks sold. Little fantasies."

But both romancers said they wrote fantasies and were proud of it. One said it was a fantasy because the heroine and hero didn't do it until the final pages. The other writer wrote historical fantasy.

Saxons, for the most part. "Lots of rape and pillage. They get it out of the way early in the romance."

The women wanted to know what she wrote.

"Not romances," Anna said. She wiped her forehead with a linen napkin. "But I do write origin stories. Little dissertations."

"Publish or Paris," Julia said. She urged oysters on Anna. Anna shook her head and felt nauseous.

After one oyster and four glasses of white wine she found herself walking again, this time while Julia held her arm on the sidewalk. Anna kept asking her where Christophe was, and how he got that way, and what he ate in the winter. Then she discreetly stumbled into a three-hundred-year-old alcove and tried to vomit but her stomach was empty and her heart. Julia waited with her hand on Anna's back and told people to mind their own bees wax when they stared. She told Anna that the bistro was boring anyway, she was just trying to impress her writers by introducing them to an intellectual. Anna said she was sure she left an impression, and they both laughed, though Anna soon began to cough instead. Julia said she loved to see this side of Paris, the part that tourists don't see. But Anna had to ask that Julia not make her laugh because she couldn't bear it, so Julia began telling her instead about the playwright she was divorcing. When Julia said their lovemaking had always been more scripted than improvised, Anna started to laugh and cough again. Then Julia asked Anna if she would like to stay in her apartment and Anna said the offer was too kind but she couldn't, not in this state. And Julia said exactly in this state. All she needed was a sleep and maybe a cry and the miracle of croissants in the morning. And in the end Anna stayed in the second bedroom and dreamed feverish scenarios of walking lost through Paris in the thirteenth century while a man like Christophe but not stalked her, and she had lost her phone and couldn't call the police.

   Tomorrow she would fly home, but now she walked through the Tuileries and vowed that next time—next time? —she would heed advice and wear heels, since nothing worked without them. She looked up and the sky above Paris was golden and aglow, as if in the heart of every man a city burned.

3. Gothic Revival

A cold wind squealed around the corner, and an autumn rain chased it down the street. Anna spun on a sensible heel. A taxi horn admonished an out-of-province license plate. Someone yelled off a balcony, something about Schopenhauer. The sidewalk traffic pulled their collars up, pulled down their hats. A cat bolted for cover from the weather. In front of *Dépanneur Victoire Sanjay* a homeless guy in a ratty fur coat and cap swayed with the gusts of wind.

Anna's house across the street was shuttered and solid against the season too, and one side abutted on a stone frat house. On her windows the blinds were thick, curtains dense. Except for that one dormer on the top floor with its flimsy lace.

Despite the rain on her neck, Anna stood fixed between her house and the corner store. She needed Sunlight soap. She'd left dirty dishes in her panic to fly to Paris. She never left dishes, but then she'd never flown to Paris before either. She didn't move from the sidewalk. Did she really want to clean as soon as she came home? But the idea was a blanket, and she wanted to snuggle up in it, and think about how clean and orderly her life would be after getting the Sunlight. And then she wondered if maybe she'd left the dishes dirty on purpose as a weird comfort, and if so then she'd known it wouldn't work out in Paris, so why hadn't she stayed home in the first place.

She'd have to walk by the homeless Sasquatch with a cigarette in its mouth. He bounced in place. The sparks from the cigarette singed the facial hair. Anna was sure she could smell wet fur from here.

She took another step towards the *dépanneur*.

The fur coat continued to bounce with an alien rhythm, partnered with furry flop ears. Yellow eyes glowed among the hair.

She took another step. The eyes turned out to be discoloured aviator glasses. They studied her house. Anna believed it all well and good that homeless schizophrenics could find shelter under the eaves of *dépanneurs*. But today wasn't a good day to be robbed. She thought herself a fine frozen target on the corner of the street, her curls sprung and makeup on the loose.

It was better to appear decisive. Anna began to rummage through what she now used as her purse, her father's satchel. But an open bag was worse. The Sasquatch began what sounded like a religious chant. Anna clutched at a found coin, held it in her fist as a fetish.

Peace and order could be bought.

She walked up the steps with her fist in front of her, but the man stepped towards the door. He flipped up one of his fur ears and withdrew a white bean from it. Anna could now hear music shout from his brain. Headphones.

"*Excusez-moi*," Anna said, her eyes on the ground.

"Radiohead," it said. A thundercloud of breath blew from his mouth.

"Anna Hill," she responded. She reached for the door.

"*Professor* Hill?" He held out his hand.

She dropped the coin into it, but the money rolled off and bounced down the steps. Then a bell chimed as she strode into Sanjay's Victorious Dépanneur.

"Small Sunlight," Sanjay said. "The dishes again."

Thank god for simple habits. Anna smiled. But there was no Sunlight on the shelves. How could there be no Sunlight? She looked outside. The homeless guy now beat the air with invisible drumsticks.

"We keep it special," Sanjay said, and waved a bottle of the soap from behind the counter.

"Wow. You're remarkable." Anna wished she could stay inside the store and let Sanjay organize her life.

"The customer comes first." He looked behind him at the curtained doorway.

"Sanjay," she said, "there's a Captain Podhead outside your door. So you know."

"Oh yes," Sanjay said. "He wears the pilot cap. Waits for someone. He has bought the farm."

Anna didn't question the phrase. Sanjay tested colloquialisms on her, unsure of their usage. Anna guessed he didn't let the homeless guy inside the store because of his wife's orders. Previous incidents of loans and reduced prices.

Anna heard Sanjay's wife now, her mumbled directives in the back room behind the curtain. "She corrects me," the storeowner said. "My favourite editor." He jiggled a pen between his fingers, balanced it on his knuckles, stuck it in his mouth.

Anna checked the front steps again. The beast was gone.

"Your novel?" she asked. She dropped her change into the bag.

Sanjay looked confused for a moment. "Right. The novel is more a screenplay now." He leaned forward. "A romantic comedy. I would like that woman from that film to be in it. I cannot remember her name, but she was in Hollywood too. Perplexingly beautiful. Unfortunately, cannot act her way out of a samosa."

"A screenplay might be easier." But then she followed Sanjay's glance outside, and saw the fur coat waddle across the street towards her house. The thing stopped in the middle of the road, bent over, turned around a few times.

"Yes. Less words."

"More money."

"It is funny how it works."

"Sanjay."

"Yes, Professor Hill."

Anna rummaged in her bag for her keys. "Could you…"

She couldn't find anything. With an abruptness that surprised her more than Sanjay, Anna dumped the satchel out onto the counter.

"Could you tell me the name of your screenplay?"

It was small change that rolled onto the wet hardwood floor, along with one pen, a plastic tampon case and some lip balm. What stayed on the counter were a glasses case, a lipstick, hair elastics, Kleenex, lipstick liner, decaf tea bag, keys! —but for her mom's house—Rescue Remedy, makeup mirror, cell phone, Band-Aid, business cards, breath strips, reading glasses out of their case, a flyer for salsa classes, a large bottle of hand cream, her chequebook, throat lozenges, and no house keys.

"It is called…*The Mango Tree Trick*," Sanjay said.

"I'm so sorry. They're here somewhere."

"Or *Small Mangos by the River House*. I'm not sure. A working progress. The story involves *fakirs*, you see. But mangos are there, definitely."

"Damn it."

"Oh dear."

Anna looked up. "I'm sorry."

"It is the wrong house."

"Your screenplay title?"

"Oh no, your friend. He goes in the house."

The vagrant stood at a front door, atop the outdoor steps.

"No no," Sanjay said through the window, "this is not your beautiful house." He waved his hand to the side.

"He's going in someone's house? Poor them."

"He has chosen wrongly."

"More than a few bad choices, I'd say. He'll go away."

"I don't think so. He is at your door."

Anna grabbed Sanjay's shoulders.

"Miss Anna," he said.

The beast turned and saw her in the window. He smiled and stretched out his fur arms, his bare palms towards them. He clapped once, then looked up in the air.

"Please call the police Sanjay." Anna fidgeted to get behind a beer ad. "He's nobody's friend."

The man caught something that fell out of the sky, held it up in a theatrical gesture.

"What's that," Sanjay said. "Something shiny."

"Oh god he's got a gun. Get down Sanjay." Anna could see her name in the paper the next day. A once peaceful neighbourhood shattered by a mythical beast. No one suspected that *Parc du Mont-Royal* had harboured the evolutionary mistake all these years. And now he'd ventured into the city to abduct a mate and destroy anyone who tried to stop him.

Sanjay looked at Anna on her knees on the wet floor. "I am sorry Professor, it is not clean. This weather makes it impossible. I will call my wife. Roopa."

"Get down." Anna pulled at his pant leg until Sanjay crouched beside her.

"It needs to be cleaned back here too. Are these your keys?"

"My mom's."

"Roopa!"

Sanjay's wife came out of back room with her broom. Her husband and the professor were crouched on the floor. It was not the first time she'd seen the professor in inexplicable positions, but it was the first time she'd seen her implicate Sanjay. Roopa hit Sanjay a few times around the legs with her broom, then began to sweep around them.

"But there's a beast," Anna said.

"Yes. He wants you to look." Roopa moved an oversized beer ad out of the way.

The fur man waved again. Then he turned to Anna's door and opened it.

"Abracadabra," said Sanjay. "I think we have found your keys."

That coin that fell on the stairs outside, that was part of a confidence trick. She knew that too well. As a child she watched the magic her dad claimed he learned in a bunker. And her mother: "Honey, give it up. You didn't fool me with those tricks the first time either. Why don't you conjure up a paycheque? That'd be a good trick, Mr. Birdman."

"Make a pony appear," Anna said.

"How about a porker," said Dotty. "We could use the bacon."

Edward reached to Anna's ear and pulled out a nickel. Again she grimaced with delight. She caught his hand and made him do it again. The sound of coins slid through her daddy's fingers all evening long.

※

The madman didn't have a gun. Otherwise Anna would never have pushed Sanjay out the door and used him as a human shield, with verbal prods from Roopa and musical accompaniment from Sanjay's doorbell.

What else could she do? In a proper époque the street person would be arrested, whipped and put in stocks. A man who wandered and hunted innocent game was sin in motion. She knew her stuff about beggars and vagabonds in medieval Europe, and without exception they met grotesque ordeals by fire and water. Theft too: if he dared pocket anything from her house, his right hand would be gone forever. Or he'd be branded—a fiery *V* on his forehead. The primary sources didn't flinch at the cruelty they meted out on the vagrant, the drifter, the outsider. Mobility brought disease and *conspirations* to overthrow the social order. They had to be stopped.

Torch-lit paranoia drove the Other from among them. They were scared for their children, their houses, their tenuous grasp on order. The vagrant cast curses on their miserly ways until a nobleman was roused from his manor, equipped with warhorse and sword and right. Able to mete out instant verdicts, he made tremble not only the vagrant but the mob that followed him, with his eyes on fire, his shoulders forward, his moustache… his moustache neatly combed.

This was justice from horseback and sword. They would fight to the death, the loser guilty. The vagrant was thrown a stick, a pole from market awnings, and between the church and bakery he faced his mismatched destiny with dread. A swing of that pole only broke it in two; another swing caught the nobleman's slice not only through the pole but also through the impudent's arm. A great bell rang across the village.

"Gothic Revival," the furry man said.

Anna pushed Sanjay's back again. "My keys," she implored.

The man said, "It looks like a castle. But it isn't."

"No, it isn't," Anna said. "But those are my keys."

"Yours maybe looks more French *château*. This one next to it is Scottish manor. Both have advantages under attack."

Anna took a few short breaths before she reached the bottom of her lungs and formed a vapour cloud above her head. Then she stood behind Sanjay and gripped his shoulders, and said, "It's Queen Anne." She squinted at the roof line. She couldn't stop herself. "Not that the Queen would have recognized it as anything she knew. And the other is Gothic Revival."

"That would explain the kids under the turret with dark trench coats, the heavy eye makeup. I will build one."

"A turret?"

"A castle."

"Good night." Anna guided Sanjay as she strode behind him up the slippery steps.

"It is a magical night. Oh, forgot to tell you," the vagrant said, and jangled a ring of cold metal. "I found your keys on the road. When you dug in your purse at the crossroads, I guess."

"I will go then," said Sanjay.

"How do you know this is my house?" She held her palm open.

"I have sources."

"I believe Roopa calls me. I will be back in the store."

"Though you know," the man said, "you don't even need keys to get into something like this. Old doors." He locked the door, pointed to a half-ton truck parked across the street with ZAP RENO painted on its door. Then he began to unbutton his fur coat and spread it wide before Anna.

An antique tool belt hung from his hips.

"It's you," Anna said.

"Always is," Zap Reno said.

"Jesus. The carpenter."

"And licensed locksmith." He plucked a tool from his belt and within ten seconds Anna's door was open again. "If you ever do lose your keys. Miracles extra."

Anna backed away from him. Rain gusted sideways. She looked at his renovation truck. Her breath formed cumulus clouds. Anna put her Rescue Remedy back in her purse, grabbed her keys from the man, and stepped through the door.

There was no duel, no ordeals for the drifter. But now at least she was inside and safe and all vagrant Sasquatches would disappear.

A wet cat snuck in her open door. "Hey!"

Zap grabbed for it, but it was already upstairs. He brushed against Anna in her doorway, smelled of wet fur and sawdust. "Hey," she said again, with as much result.

"He likes you," Zap said on the way out, the cat flopped over his shoulder. "Good thing. He'll come and visit." Before Anna could close the door completely he said, "We're next door. We bought the Gothic."

4. Woman in Jeopardy

There was a memo marked urgent on her desk when Anna got back. *While You Were Out*, it read, Dmitri had come to her office, wanted to see her. The history department secretary clung to the nostalgia of paper memos. Aside from the distinct spice of pepper, the entire floor reeked of irony.

Anna went to see the Chair.

"Right, Anna. A matter with your class."

"Okay."

"Paris was helpful?"

I want a refund on Paris, she wanted to say, but didn't. She wanted to say, Next time she'd opt for an on-line conference.

"I won't lie," Anna said, "I made a fabulous entry."

"I can imagine. Your assistant, meanwhile."

"I was…Audrey?"

"Is full of energy. Always organizes."

"I get dizzy," said Anna.

"Yes well. You had better sit down. She organized while you were out."

"That's what she's paid for. Though not much."

"So we hear." Dmitri directed her again to a chair full of books. Anna picked them up and put them on her lap with the care of a Shih Tzu trainer.

"It began with a door," Dmitri said.
"As these things do."

Everything was cool until Audrey reached the classroom door, but things quickly deteriorated when her bag of books and uncooperative scarf blocked her view.

"Let me get that," a student said.

"Pardon?" Audrey said.

The boy reached in front of her and turned the doorknob. He pushed it open.

Audrey couldn't move.

"After you," the boy said.

"I can open a door I think," she said.

"I take all your classes."

"Please close the door."

"Do you get nervous in front of a crowd?"

"You should be nervous right now."

"I imagine everyone in their underwear."

Audrey threw up her hands. Several books fell across the hallway.

"I mean not like that," he said.

"It was from that point," Dmitri said, "that your assistant refused to enter the room, and began to teach the class from the hallway."

"Always resourceful."

"This attracted some attention."

"I can assure you Dmitri," Anna started.

"...as the theme of the lesson that afternoon was the long-awaited death of chivalry."

"So forty years ago."

"Or six centuries. A truffle occurred."

"I see."

"Between two boys."

"You don't mean a tussle, surely."

"This one. Boys were led to the fisticuffs over ideology."

For years Anna had taught the thrills and spills of History with the full intention of provoking a reaction from her students. Never once had a brawl broken out over her methodologies.

"No one was hurt?"

"Security was there. Complaints about noise already made. Boys peacocked."

"Thank god for peacocks. So that was it?"

"Of course, this tassel only drew more people."

"Ah."

"Audrey took the opportunity to instruct the entire floor, which, I refer to a student's notes I have, first veered toward freedom of speech. As these things do." Dmitri Bushnov adjusted his tie.

"Youth," Anna said.

"And then a sharp left turn towards the dilemma of abysmal Teachers' Assistants' salaries."

"Neither the place nor time. But then everyone went home?"

"Then without much further prompt, she began to organize."

Anna winced. "Not that nature deficit disorder she goes on about?"

"She was ready to march them up Mount Royal, say our sources. Only there was snow. The slush. Winter happened since you left. Somehow—the record here is sketchy—lack of interest in outdoor history lessons led her to attempt a walk-out protest for the entire history department."

"She doesn't look it, but she's a passionate thing."

"She does look it. In my day, they would have *gulaged* her."

Or made a statue of her, Anna thought. In the day. She didn't find it difficult to imagine a marble Audrey eager to point out the future in a public square.

"I don't need to go on, yes?"

"Yes," Anna said. Clearly, nobody saw Anna with tenure in her future. At least she had that research grant coming up. Maybe she'd be able to escape to a dark library in Spain.

"As it is, she has been temporarily suspended. Only because there is an official complaint. Numbers of sexual harassment charges are bandied about our halls." He quoted: "The effect of which impairs that person's work or educational performance where it is known—or ought to be known—that the conduct is unwelcome."

"I need her," Anna blurted.

Dmitri nodded. "Protocol is necessary. They like the protocol. Exoneration of the respondent. Form A-09, Vexatious Behaviour. All unpleasant." He smiled for the first time.

"What was the complaint?"

"I cannot say with assurance, only to say it was a boy. We have to investigate the romantic attachment accusations."

"As these things do," Anna said.

Anna stood up from her computer and forgot why she had come to the kitchen.

She took off her sweater. Botticelli nymphs danced on her refrigerator, a postcard from Audrey. Who still sent postcards?

Most of her international correspondence came from her assistant. In the Uffizi basement, this last visit. A restorer boyfriend. Grey around the edges and only spoke Italian but otherwise functional, Audrey informed her, and Anna turned her ears aside. But next to Audrey's postcard now was one she'd brought back herself, from Paris. A turn-of-the-century postcard of the new Eiffel Tower, with a boxy biplane in flight over it. Not as garish as Audrey's.

Anna opened the refrigerator door. She looked inside blankly, closed it, opened it again. The dishes were done.

"Tea," she said. She took out the milk and left the door open for a good thirty seconds before a cool draft reminded her.

At her desk, the wisps of steam from her teapot only brought back *des cafés terrasses*, of cobbled streets in morning fog, of the misty things that might have been. But she got to work. She studied a list of all the body parts mentioned in *Tristan und Isolde*, and how they were mentioned without gender, and how collar bones and throats got particular attention, being some of the few erogenous zones ever spotted at medieval parties. Then she realized her computer screen was steamed from the tea.

Outside, the early snows of October fell wet and thick.

Life beguiled more than any words she could fit on the screen. Pigeons filled the window. Behind them, a young sunset brushed Mount Royal, coloured the trees now dipped in cloud dust. At six o'clock. Like that sunset she saw from the Pont des Arts, across from the Louvre. And it was still too hot at her desk. The air was old in this stuffy room. She got up to try the ancient window again, but needed something to prop it up. She picked up the closest book—no, that one she might need. She picked up another and began to look through it, checked it didn't have any notes of remarkable insight or expository clarity wedged among its otherwise grey pages. Then she read it, a small section on courtly love as an eroticization of nobility, because there was something there that could tweak her paper. The light from the snow reflected on the book, with the rare and perfect intrusion every few minutes of sun blinks through the imperfect blown-glass window. All its distortions conspired to create a dance of ultraviolet on the page, to make this author's ponderous text brighten, literally, and come alive, and this was the thing for her paper, she had it now, there.

A dull crack sounded through the wall. Anna looked around, but she wasn't too surprised. The house shifted and cracked in arctic lows, protested as much as Anna.

She sat back down in front of the screen and studied her words but thought of Paris. And she forgot all the pages she had read in that illuminated book, and instead she wrote,

> He saw me from across the room. His glance told me to stay where I was and not move. I couldn't anyway. He waved a necklace. I was unable to get out of the bed, and when I tried I limped so badly I fell to the tiles.
>
> "I am the Falconer," he told me. His horse stayed where it was without a command.
>
> In a disused Spanish monastery, filled with Andalusian horses, hares, wild boars digging up trees and truffles, swallows in the courtyards, and mourning doves, rain fell on the empty fountain tiles.

Anna found herself a little breathless. Words came too easy, like theft from the blind. And they came with matched baggage, a shady guilt. Historical romance appeared to need little more than a few upswept capes, a horse and some vague past. Julia on the plane, she'd quoted Flaubert, of all people—his desire to escape "inside a subject of splendour." Well. If romance editors could fly around and quote Flaubert, Professor Anna Hill could go around and plot sexual tension. She was a little concerned at how a horse got into a monastery bedroom, more so than how the girl had got there. After a little reflection she thought it best to leave them both there for now. But where had the heroine got that terrible limp?

Anna tapped a pen on her forehead until she had something of a tattoo in spilled ink. A limp would need a cane. Did heroines use canes?

Her fingers lay on the keyboard. A letter repeated itself thirteen times before she noticed. jjjjjjjjjjjjj. Distant taps. Like some students in her history class who typed out their lives online. The taps regular like a cane, but a cane that navigated a cobblestone street. In Spain.

> A woman did not go unnoticed in Las Naranjas. A young woman with egotistical red hair was an apparition. And a young woman with a cane, tap-tapping her way through the cobblestones—my appearance would become legendary. And entirely unforgettable for him, Florio.

Where had that come from? *Florio?* Was that even a name?

> I did not walk in beauty like the night—my cane was a spotlight. The appearance of Scottish hair in a Spanish monastery—disused or not—and my tap-tap-tapping of it, mocking the Andalusian dances, lit my entry and burnt it on the minds of both caliphs and slaves forever.
>
> There have been various canes carved and stolen for me. They have sat in a corner of my rock-hewn bedroom, beside the grand fireplace. I will only use one, even though I admire the handiwork of my courters—the twists of the branches, the nods

to antiquity of Grandfather's cane. Beasts and flora burst from the tops. A museum of Spain takes root in that corner.

Anna looked behind her. She had to print this out and study it later. Nobody watched her write this stuff. She could do this all afternoon and nobody had to know. The printer oozed out the pages, and she quickly scooped them together. Aside from the soup of past, present and future tenses, it read all right. Compared to other romances. None of which she had read. Except for the one. Saw it at the Montreal airport bookstore when she finally escaped Paris. Bought it. *For research.* She breezed through it, then inserted it in a pile of academic discourses. Now she found it again.

She stood up in front of the window and pulled out the thick romance. Another crack from the roof made her jump. Maybe the hot room was too much of a contrast for the frozen roof. She wrenched open the window one more time and wedged the book underneath it.

Another crack exploded next to her ear. Anna jumped away from the wall. The pigeons flew away too. On the thick single pane a circle of snow clung to a corner, and patiently began its descent. She inched toward the window. Maybe the new roof snow melted in the sporadic sun. She looked up outside, but saw nothing. And one more time she wrenched the old window further up, picked up the book, enough to worry her head out and hold the window with her shoulder. Sometimes these roofs collapsed.

The next snowball hit above her ear.

She may have screamed, she couldn't say, but the shock made her forget the window, and it squeezed down on her shoulder. She was pinned with her head and shoulders and one arm out the window in pigeon poop three stories above the earth, ready for her roof to cave in, her article unedited, no make-up, hair unwashed (after she discovered she'd used conditioner as shampoo in Paris the whole time), and to her surprise, a ponderous romance novel still in hand.

"Hey!"

Now people yelled at her.

"Professor Anna Hill?"

It was the neighbour. With his disastrous timing and worse raccoon coat. "Go away," Anna whispered, and waved the book. A few students stopped and gaped at where Zap stared. The young mouths hung open as if the words they knew were too laden with knowledge. But slight clouds of breath floated from their lips and swirled to Anna's window. Snow began to sneak down her cheekbones. What lunatic had thrown a snowball at her?

"Jackson Zaporzan," he said. His voice boomed up three floors. "More commonly Zap. We broke into your house together."

"Oh brother," she said.

"Your Gothic neighbour. Have they locked you in the attic?"

Huge flakes landed on her neck, bit her with a thousand frozen teeth.

"I need some air. I have to go in now. Goodbye."

Zap grinned through his beard. "I need to talk to you about the house." He looked up at her, at her turret. Her hair was a red blossom on an ivy wall. A squirrel's tail hanging from a tree.

"What do you see," Anna said.

"Your tower."

"Why my tower?"

"It's fallen apart. Your cornices are critical, your slate tiles have slipped, and one of these days they'll knock out a student. You'll want to avoid those kinds of lawsuits." Zap flipped a coin in his hand.

"Slate?" Anna said. She regretted it. "Stop," she said. "Don't tell me. All right? My head is frozen. I refuse to get hypothermia in my own house. I'll wriggle back inside now. In the future you could use a telephone like the majority of Western civilization. Goodbye."

Anna went nowhere.

"Would you prefer," Zap shouted, in the middle of the intersection beside the house, "that I call the fire department, or if your door is open should I ascend into your turret?"

Anna didn't answer. No one had ever asked her that before. She gave a push towards the window, and tried to slip sideways. But she didn't get back into the house, and only managed to give herself deeper scratches on her caught arm.

Zap watched as her free arm flapped the book in the air.

"Maybe you should let that book drop. Your arm's gonna fall off. You might need it to push up the window."

Lovely. The new neighbour was a born stage manager. A controller, a director: a man.

Anna pushed up with her back on the window. Nothing. Except a pain burned up her spine. She expressed it out loud.

"What?" Zap asked.

"I'm…" Now the book weighed forty pounds. Soon she would cry. With a crowd below. Her tears dangerous icicles.

"Drop the book."

"I can't."

"I'll catch ya."

"I need it. I found a reference I can use." The last said for the benefit of the student crowd gathered underneath her turret. A girl pointed her cell phone at her, took a picture. Had he said catch *you*?

"What page?"

Anna was sure her eyelashes were stuck together. And her neck itched. Where the snow melted.

"What page is the reference? I'll mark it after you drop it."

She lifted the book to scratch her neck. Why she had chosen such an immense romance she couldn't imagine. She still confused weighty with serious. Her neck felt better with the book on it. But now the arm twisted behind her head was tired.

"Is that yoga?"

She had to stretch her arm now before it cramped. She let the book rest on her shoulder, held it there with her head and let her arm stretch. The book slipped. Her hand shot back to hold it, caught it by the inside pages. Her fingers wet and cold. If she couldn't move, neither could the book. She flipped it, caught it by the covers. Smiled. And with a good twist that aggravated her back and arm and neck, she lay the book on the snowy windowsill.

"You can all go home now," Anna said. "The show is over."

On top of the mountain, the sun blipped and disappeared. A gentle wind blew a swirl of snow onto Anna's face. The pigeons on the next window leapt into the air a made a little snowstorm of their own. One landed on her windowsill.

Anna screamed.

"That's my girl," Zap said. He called out to the bird.

Perfect. Frozen in her own home, her eyes pecked out by a pigeon. Ghastly photographs posted by some student.

"Shoo. Shoo."

The bird shuffled away, jumped on top of the book. The romance jiggled but didn't slip. But now the pigeon wanted to come inside the house. Anna shouted at the thing, waved her free arm, hit the book. The pigeon flew off, but now the book waltzed on the snow, made two rotations before it teetered on the edge, then began to fall.

With her last frustrated bit of strength, Anna made a grab for it, caught one page. "Ha," she said.

"Lot of work for one book," Zap commented. The students around him murmured about the relative merits of literature.

It was a big book. The page began to tear.

"No!"

She watched it tear. She watched her reputation tear all the way down the side of the page. And then it was free. The book flapped its pages like a baby bird kicked from the nest. Anna felt her stomach lighten. The receipt from the bookstore escaped, a loose feather. Six excited pigeons took off from another windowsill. And then, with a thud, the book landed in a pile of slush beside the crowd. A car splash added to its misery. A student fished it out and wiped the glossy cover on his parka sleeve.

"*The Dragon's Breast* ?" he said.

"Page one hundred and sixty-nine," Anna called out while she waved her strip of torn paper. "It's a deconstruction of the parameters of romance." It didn't sound as scholarly as she had hoped. She swore to abandon her Falconer forevermore.

5. Special Operations

Her mother at her suburban doorstep: pulled up the collar of her cardigan, tucked a bottle of furniture polish under her arm.

"Squirrely," Dotty said. "Nutty as a fruitcake."

She'd told Anna to rush over. To meet an Auntie Pearl she'd never seen, who'd moved back to town.

"Oh she can be pleasant to have tea with, if you can ever figure out what she says," Dotty said.

But the aunt was gone already, Anna was too late.

"She romances her life. I never heard her tell a straight story. And that was before her wires started to short-circuit and they put her in this Assisted Life Centre."

Anna was sure she had room in her agenda for those higher altitudes peculiar to Alzheimer's patients or the blissfully senile. She'd looked for a volunteer cause since last year, but still hadn't found the right one. "I could go say hi," she said.

"You'll find scrambled eggs, over easy. But," Dotty said, and her voice dipped a few notes. "She is our burden. Every family, they have one member with a tenuous link to reality. *L'artiste de la famille*, like your French friends say. She's ours."

"My French friends?"

"Don't get her on the Mosquitoes," Dotty said. "She claims she flew with the Fairy Commandos."

"I'll put some coffee on."

"The worst rumours are the ones we spread about ourselves," Dotty said. She didn't elaborate, but waited for her daughter to offer any news of herself.

They sat in the nook for an hour. They always took their coffee breaks there. Dotty started after Babyboy Quince was old enough to sleep through them. Back then she sat there alone and gazed out the window, watched Anna dig up her garden, the flowers intact. She always tried to unearth something. Dotty let her. The garden wasn't Dotty's obsession. She hated the dirt. Claimed she'd always been an eco-gardener. Believed the earth was better left to its own devices, to decompose what lay beneath.

"I'm sorry you missed her. She had to rush off. The busiest woman I know." Dotty pointed to her couch. A plastic leg reclined on the cushions.

"She looks like you said."

"Don't be a goose. She forgot it, poor dear. Loses it around the edges."

Anna nodded with enforced seriousness. She rolled her head, waited for a crack of the neck bones. Sometimes it took forever. At her mother's she could roll for hours. This time her neck clicked almost immediately.

"Today she kept repeating, 'Never date a man in Special Operations,'" her mother said. "Oh, she tells wonderful stories. Spies, fairies, the Gravity Machine."

"Sorry?"

"Your auntie. Wonderful histories. An unpredictable past."

Anna was reminded of where she'd inherited her historian's skepticism.

"But she's lonely. Doesn't have a man. Never did as far as we know. I told her you'd be there for her eighty-seventh birthday. Next Saturday."

"Halloween?" Anna said. "I'm invited somewhere already." But she had nothing that weekend. Only an idea about dressing up in costume again, knocking on Christophe's door, and confronting him about the Paris conference. The nun thing had worked the first time. Almost.

Her mother poured coffee. Added her splash of Bailey's Irish Cream, and watched Anna silently plot. "You could maybe learn something from your spinster aunt," she said. "Who is sad and alone."

From the end of a dark hallway Otto the pug waddled into view. He headed for Anna.

"Otto's well," Anna said.

Dotty sprayed the lemon polish toward the dog as it shuffled by. "At least he smells better. Counters the glands."

Halloween and till this moment she'd completely forgotten about walking the aunt. And her nun's habit still stained with wine and brie. The more the day went on the stupider the idea of showing up at Christophe's door in costume seemed, until by evening, after the few neighbour children struggled by in costumes hidden by parkas and snow boots, and the college girls shivered down sidewalks in their sexy anything costumes, she abandoned the idea. Instead Anna pulled on flannel pyjama top and bottom and wool socks, and with a sigh planted herself in front of her vanity to remove her mask of make-up.

Of course, he could show up at the door. She'd left a note on his office door, cryptic yet unequivocal: "We have to talk about Paris. – AH." He could ring the bell—she'd replaced the buzzer with a more ecclesiastical tone recently—and she would say what a surprise it was, and what the cat dragged in, and wasn't it so.

And then he would kiss her, authentically.

And she would take that as an apology, a confession, hell, she'd take it as a prayer.

But she would shake her head. She had to go push her wheelchair-bound aunt. Nobody else took care of the poor thing and she needed air, cold and restorative. She would unsheathe her double-edge sword: sexy *and* altruistic, but she didn't drop everything for the first man who kissed her.

And then her bell chimed.

Kids could be at her door this unholy night, but none had rung yet, and it was late for children. She thought she heard chants downstairs.

But the bell: he had come!

Except now she was in pyjamas and her make-up incomplete. She opened a window and from the draperies called "*J'arrive.*"

She splashed more water on her eyes and made a quick pass with the remover, and a new stroke of the liner on her eyebrows and a lipstick...but she couldn't find the good colour now, the one that Audrey liked on her, just pink enough for healthy but not slutty. She undid her hair from a bun and slipped on a bandana that let her red hair bounce as she walked, and tried one jewel on her neck, probably not, not with pyjamas...there it was the lipstick, the Mac one, she painted it on with a touch of red overlay. The pyjamas were flirty enough, but she pulled off the wool socks as she started to pad down the cold steps, threw them up to the kitchen, took short breaths, which made her dizzy and she reached for the railing, luckily the toes painted yesterday for god knows what reason, and near the bottom slowed to creak down each step to make sure whoever waited on the other side of the door could hear her arrive with care and assurance and *savoir-faire*. She grabbed a scarf that hung on the door knob and the small metal bowl of candy she'd left there just in case.

She would not let him kiss her. How the French women did it. She swung the door open.

No one was there. A small brown-paper package. She bent to pick it up, and halfway down thought better of it. A Halloween trick.

"Arrgh!"

The man was behind the door. He did not usually set out to frighten women who lived alone, as he found the target too broad and the reception, ever since he'd been shot at that time in New Orleans, too risky. But he wasn't there to scare the professor so much as to surprise and delight her. Maybe he'd hid too well, or his Arrgh was too authentic. All the same, he was the one delighted when she stood up and launched a bowl of Lindt chocolates into his hands.

He was on fire, which may also have accounted for her alarm. Also, he sang snatches of rum soaked songs, and fake dreadlocks sprang from his pirate's hat, and from his unkempt beard birthday cake sparklers threw golden stars.

"Arrgh! Thank you for the classy chocolates. Take a while to find the door, don't you?"

It was Jackson Zaporzan. Anna patted down her pyjama top as the sparklers continued to attack. Zap had wondered if she might be in costume, and was about to guess who she was supposed to be, with her flannel clothes and the kind of messy ghoul kohl around her eyes, but before he could say anything there was a small explosion and she jumped back again. The rest of the chocolates spilled down the outside stairs. Zap caught a few more, but then more explosions followed—the sparks had ignited the string of firecrackers tied to his beard.

"Arrgh," he claimed. "I'm Bluebeard, and here to kidnap you aboard my ship."

But the firecrackers and sparklers were too close to his face and he covered his eyes, and soon the beard glowed a little too much, and on one side a small flame appeared, and in seconds his chin was alight. Anna unfurled her scarf and smothered his face. Smoke curled around them.

He bent to pick up the package and took the scarf, rubbed his beard thoroughly. "That is a disappointment. I don't know how Bluebeard did this."

Showing up at her door in costume had sounded like a wiser idea the more he thought about it, and after some research he was positive that Anna's interest in dragons and romances would naturally attract her to pirates.

Zap stood still as the professor took back her ruined scarf from his hands. Although his dreadlocks were hardened and his beard almost all gone, and although the smell of singed hair settled between them, he thought he'd made a lasting impression. She hadn't run away, or aimed a pistol at him, so that was a start. She wrinkled her tiny nose. Maybe she smelled the sea salt spray on the pirate's ship, brought by the trade winds that wrapped her dress around her legs. Battles at sea were full of danger. A woman like her needed a man, unafraid and free, more than these modern, effete pirates. He reached out his hand to her, felt at her temples to search for the singed ends of her own red hair. He brought it to his nose, then rubbed the remains down the front of his blackened shirt, then looked closer at her skin, felt for blisters, found none, dipped his fingers in the condensation on the door window and tried to wipe clean her face.

"Bluebeard wasn't a pirate," Anna said. "You mean Blackbeard." She pulled back from him.

But his hands continued to hold her face, until he was convinced she was unhurt, until Anna's eyes focused again and came back from the sea.

"You're in love," he said.

Anna buttoned the top of her pyjamas around her neck.

"With this house. With your turret."

I am not that obvious, Anna thought. I am not desperate.

"It is a charming house. Like mine. But you have to get out. Now. The whole thing is about to crumble. Look at this." He unwrapped part of the package and showed her a broken square of roof slate. "You're not safe here."

"That's obvious. I'll call the fire department. Or the police." Anna started to close the door.

"Whoa, whoa. Police don't repair roofs. You need emergency intervention renovation. Are those pyjamas?"

"Yes they're pyjamas."

"They are so you. Good costume. Brings out the red in your hair."

Anna realized she was freezing out here.

"Got a present for you too. Halloween present. It's a book on castle building." He pulled it out of the package. "You're welcome. But there's something else bothering you."

"The self-immolation on my doorstep?"

"I want to help."

"I don't need that kind of help." She looked at the book. Ages nine and up. Lavishly illustrated. She looked at the ceiling, and one side of her lips smiled.

"Stop that," Zap said. "You kill me with that look."

He took a step and the wood floor protested. Anna backed up.

"But these timbers creak. Installed in the industrial revolution. Your door doesn't close right. A few things to repair, you come back when it's done, but you should get out now. I mean, you don't know the kooks in this neighbourhood."

She wasn't aware she had a Look.

"I can do a quick fix on the roof before more snow."

"Alone in my house."

"If you like. But I wouldn't be alone. I'll bring a crew."

"It's cold. With the door open."

"You see? Twisted frame. Your hydro bills will strangle you." He took another step. "So, roof, a few nails in the stairs, tweak the outside door. Do it in a weekend."

"So why would I leave?"

"A noisy job. You can take it like a holiday. Look at what bothers you. When the reno's finished you can be logical again." Zap bounced on the step, made it sing an ode to its homeland forest.

"I do need some repairs," she said.

He brought out a crumpled business card. "This is the only one I've got, so if you could give it back when you're done."

"I know where you live."

Zap nodded.

"But I'll do it at my own pace."

"Sure you will."

"So I'll knock on the wall…Mister…is this your name? Zap Reno? Or your business? Mr. Zaporzan. When I'm ready. Here's the deal though. You have to recognize my personal space."

"Oh yeah, I recognize it."

Anna held her pyjamas at the neck. What Look?

"Impossible to miss. You got a galaxy of space here."

6. You Have Pomegranate Juice on Your Chin There

Now the opera arrived on the wings of snow sirens from the arctic. They sang for her, the tow trucks and plows under the street lamps at dawn. Chorus with tuques low and scarves high, Nordic burqas. The arias of spinning tires on ice, the crescendo of cars rocking forward, backward, searching for traction. They invaded her dreams until she woke to find her scenery frozen, its corners rounded and its colours erased by monotone white.

Anna wore a white blouse. In her university office hung spare white shirts. She arrived damp with the effort of negotiating uncleared sidewalks and put on a fresh one. Down the university's marble hallway she wove, with starts and stops, spun when she heard echoing voices. She used to walk down this hallway with purpose, move from point A (her office) to point B (the classroom) without interruption, with full concentration on her next class. But now the students' whispers screamed like seagulls. Doors opened—she glanced—not the right people—doors closed. She stopped in front of faded photos of Deans in the 1930s, became wistful and melancholic beside marble columns. Every other day she could navigate the way to her classroom. To the end, turn left. But today's hallway stretched out further with every step, as if Anna she still lived in the fluid architecture of dreams, or suffered the hallucinations of a sleep-deprived prisoner in solitary. Though that she could do. Six months without interruptions, without neighbours or aunts or cats. A guardian to slide up a tiny door and push her a bowl of broth for sustenance. That's all she needed: a vacation. And she would write. She would concoct the most baroque Romance a woman would ever need, with love and tenderness and uncountable shades of sex.

Anna's boot heels tapped a beat, and she straightened her trajectory to the classroom. She was flamenco and fire and grace, she brought warmth to the marble, melted the ice sheets outside.

Her romance heroine would not leave her. She would give up on Christophe. She would write the Romance and, despite the odds, the heroine would be a Medieval Spanish nun. Anna already felt herself a better person. The nun's influence.

"Anna."

She spun, her hair bobbed in slow motion around her. The students' cries turned to choirs of praise. But it was only Dmitri.

"My God, professor. You cannot walk alone like this. You will soon trail the parade of broken hearts. I will protect you."

His rotund charm slowed her pace. Her own heart felt elastic, stretched at the sound of her name, snapped back when it was not the man she had sought since Paris.

"Mit'ka."

They stopped while Dmitri shook his head, then studied the marble floor. "With buckwheat," he said finally. "And topped with chopped smoked salmon, little onion, chopped eggs, sour cream." He looked up at Anna, his eyes moist, unfocused on a distant past. He had a young woman's lips and an old woman's moles.

"At the end of my day in school, mother would wrap this up, wrap me up. In the evenings, father would let me sneak sips from his bottle. After the walk home, the cold brisk and clean, like today. Do you not love it?"

Anna made an expression that she hoped look broad and eager. But it was fortified with irony.

"My parents they hated nature. Pined for Moscow. I could only play in secret outside in winter. Taught myself to ski on scraps of vodka barrel."

Anna lost her concentration again. *Dr. Zhivago* danced in her head, although she tried everything to send him away. She looked straight at Dmitri, who looked straight at the floor, but all she could see was Omar Sharif cradling Julie Christie in his arms, both of them befurred and befuddled on a sleigh to nowhere. Could she give up Christophe like that, after wolves howled around their ice palace, after forces larger than they tore them apart?

Dmitri brushed a trail of black breadcrumbs from one side of his sweater. Word was his ex-wife had left him shortly after the collapse of the Soviet.

"Of course, we must touch on the business with your TA," he began.

"Oh right."

"But in the meantime, next week, there will be outing."

Anna pictured Omar Sharif coaxed out of a closet.

"A little Nordic ski trip. Frolic in the snow. Delight in nature. Like that. In the Laurentians. I invite you."

Dmitri reached out to caress her shoulder, thought better of it, and instead waved at a student. His hand accidentally brushed against Anna's curls anyway, and for a second he held his fingers under his nose in contemplation.

"I don't know how to ski."

His eyes widened. They made his already round face into a kindly blowfish.

Anna bit her lip to stop a smile. Dr. Zhivago had left long ago on his sleigh.

"When can I expect to have Audrey back, Mit'ka?"

"Everybody skis. You are from Quebec. Après-ski. I know how you like to have a good time." He said this to her shoes.

She looked at the ceiling. Between her and Dmitri they saw everything.

"We will get you out of gym," Dmitri said. "Sometimes you have to get off your treadmill and into wildlife."

Was he flirting with her? It didn't matter. Anna shook her head. "There's no way…"

"The French man comes as well."

"There's no way I'd miss it."

7. There Will Be Love

"Christophe?"

The snow comes at her sideways, from above, from below, finds every gap in her clothes, mocks her attempts to shield her face. The woolen scarf over her nose is an ice fort.

"Dmitri?"

The truth is she hates to ski.

"Thorbert?"

She isn't so enamored of nature right now either.

Anna ponders a river frozen in its bed. No ski tracks are on it except for her hatched attempt. And those disappear fast. Like the sketched skiers in front of her, now erased into a blank page.

She still can't figure out how it happened. Sure, she was slower than the others in the woods. And she realized she had stared at the furrows beneath her feet the whole time, hypnotized by the scrape of the skis, only occasionally registering the others' commentary about animal tracks. The only thing worth a look was Christophe's form, which she could learn from and incorporate into her own technique. But he was always over a hillock or past a bend, lustful in his pursuit of the New World, eager to eclipse the Norwegian. Between debates about the provenance of snow-dusted animal scat, she missed the discussion about a planned route.

And yes she'd wobbled more than necessary, and fell three times before she arrived at an actual trail. The equipment bought thirteen years ago to impress some rocky Scandinavian who'd asked if she enjoyed Nordic pursuits. He'd snagged her with the capitalized word, led her imagination down the path of solid men with blonde hair on extravagant polar bear rugs.

She'd never used the skis. Not once. She couldn't get them into her car, never mind onto her feet.

So her one snare to lure Christophe was dysfunctional. The preparation was rushed, and her ski style was not to her advantage. If she were an athlete, Anna believed, she would help someone who wasn't *au courant*. An arm held for balance, for example, got you over that initial curve. A hand to guide the calf in the proper push. The brush of fingers over a bare shoulder. That would be for the *après*. But she'd lost the French man before they'd left the parking lot.

She should have known when she passed the last McDonald's before the wilderness. Or when she discovered most of the faculty invitees had sensibly canceled. Only Dmitri waited beside his car, struggled with dated Russian equipment, revelled in the conditions, still in sweater and dress shirt underneath his unzipped parka.

"Do not worry about me," he said. Blood stained his teeth. Anna winced. Somehow he'd hurt his lip already, and he was only at his leather boots. "In Russia, this is Sunday afternoon in park with George. This is comedy musical." He smiled red. She said nothing to encourage him. She'd tried to stop Dmitri before. Tried to stop a masochist's complaints with a whip. The Chair of History was aglow. He would glean months of misery material for conversation.

"Like the Mother Country makes," he said, and rubbed his bare hands together, his boots now fastened, his face aflame. How could his roundness cavort through these hills?

"Is there anyone else?"

"Only obsessive-compulsives. They're on a test run. There. That's Thorbert, our trusty guide. And Native woman."

Anna watched a blur of black emerge from the woods, eventually discernible as three figures. If he wasn't among them, she would turn back right now.

"Our French colleague the only other brave enough, I guess."

Anna recognized his cantered stride, the easy way he moved through the world. He'd grown up on skis, weaned on holidays in Chamonix, all *après* and cocktails and furry boots. Tanned, rugged faces. Mountain climbs to discover medieval monasteries. The camaraderie of explorers. Fireplaces, hot mulled wine. Confessions. The brush of fingers.

"Your car door, you left it open."

Anna shivered.

Thorbert glided towards Anna. A gadget freak. Like he was ready to scuba dive. Everything matched and tight. While she struggled with her baggy pants and zipped-up down parka. A quick repair job lingered around her arm, black electric tape to keep in errant feathers.

"You are mourning?" Thorbert asked.

Everyone's cheeks were already red.

"You have come alone?"

"I'm a single girl. All alone in a great big world." She watched Christophe race The Native Woman in her peripheral vision.

"It is not possible."

"Oh it's possible. I work at it. Yourself?"

But the two others slid beside them, the dark woman with a pale laugh.

"These are not my ski," said Christophe, for he arrived a metre behind her. "A woman waxed them this morning in the shop who did not know what she did. I am sticky, not swishy. I should be swishy."

"We should all be swishy," the woman said. Diane Silverbow she called herself. A fringed leather coat. Pocahontas, from the costume party. More like Madonna Thunderhawk. Black tights outlined her young calves and thighs that never touched. Behind her, Christophe pulled up his mountaineer goggles. He still caught his breath. They looked like newlyweds. The snow their confetti.

The last time Anna had seen such thick snow was when she fell in love with the new neighbour boy who stood outside in his yard and caught flakes on his tongue. Until his knit tuque fell off and she saw he was a girl. Her twilight of gender.

Now she shivers again, alone. Her glasses are fogged and ice-crusted, useless. She puts them in a pocket. Above her the hungry roar of a jet prepares to descend upon Montreal. People don't freeze to death below airport flight paths. After the noise subsides, she listens through the wind. Must be back over the river. She wiggles her toes in her boots, can still feel them. She moves one ski forward and it glides underneath the river ice into a trough of slush.

"Hey guys!" she tries. "I'm here."

But nothing moves. She yanks her foot back in a panic. The ski tip claws underneath the ice. More shivers. She will be frozen to the spot, drive-thru for wildlife. The water feels transgressive in her boot. She pulls harder, and falls back onto the snow. Anna takes off her gloves and puts both hands under the ice to unfasten the boot from the ski. In a few seconds she pulls her hands out again, unsuccessful. She claps them together, blows on them, plunges them in the water again. Fumbles with her laces, slides her foot out of the boot, kicks it away. She watches the ski and boot bubble into the grey of the river's belly.

No time to wonder. She pulls off her soaked wool sock, twists it till no more water drips off, then slides it back on again, a cold comfort. Her foot burns. Off comes the sock, and instead her Peruvian toque goes over her foot. She fishes in pockets until her numb fingers find a hair elastic. Slides it over the toque and lets it bite into her ankle. As she fishes she paws at her phone, something she should have done long ago. The battery is weak but alive. But there are no bars in this wilderness. Anna takes one step and her unskied foot sinks three feet into the snow. When she pulls it out her tuque is gone.

That's her sock sunk goodbye in the water. Anna falls backwards again, and the snow catches her. Her legs pull to her belly. Squirrels of red hair nestle her cheeks. The naked foot rises into the wind. Christophe would hold it in his paws. Only them, two natural-born healers. Her toes warm already as he massages. Words of comfort through the lips of a foreign tongue.

And then, with the nerve to make a guest appearance in her delirium, that Native woman. Looks over the shoulder of Christophe, guides his hands, plucks herbs and enchantments from a fringed satchel.

The vision is enough to shake Anna out of her reverie. Her foot jerks on muscle memory, digs into her other leg. The other leg hardly notices.

She manages a smile though: she is happy to have worn her baggiest and heaviest clothing, dressing in layers perhaps the one eternal thing her father had taught her. Black tights were no help in a blizzard. And this puffy jacket thing, that was back in style, wasn't it? The Seventies? She calculates eras by instinct. Is that the limbo zone of hipness? Thirty-eight years? In nineteen-seventy she was three years old. She rubs her foot. In nineteen-seventy her father and his layers flew away. She ought to get into the bush, out of the wind that carried sounds. What might be a pigeon. Or an owl. Pigeons are for cities, like professors. No matter what they wear.

Anna shivers again. She knows she should move, not ice up on the riverbank. But there is something comfortable when she lets go. When she is left.

On her back, she avoids the worst of it. The wind howls at the bent fir and pine tops, loses its voice in the clearing. A crow calls, that she recognizes. Warns others of her? The bird is frozen in the air above her, points into the wind and doesn't advance. Where does it go?

Against the grey sky, a cloud emerges. Condensed breath from a god's cough. The wind comes in ragged exhales now, in the silences the storm inhales more force. Iced trees clear their throats in the woods. But the snow has stopped. Anna sits up. Another cough blows at her face, tears salt from her eyes. A snap—this one almost above her head—and she turns to see a six-foot branch land in the snow beside her, its viscera exposed, moist with recent life.

Without intent Anna is already twenty feet from the tree. She hasn't noticed how she got her last ski off and cut through the snow banks, nor has she heard her panicked breaths, or the faint call on the wind. She bends over, feels her foot, now takes stock of her breath, slows it down. And the call, a whisper that fights the wind with the frozen crow. Christophe has a high-pitched voice like that. Christophe has not deserted her. The call comes again, but this time it's not him, can't be. A dog's wail, chained and lonely. She wants to sit down again. But a dog, if there's a dog there's a master. She yowls back at it. The thing answers, lonelier. But not alone. Other dogs are with it. Anna stumbles towards the sound. Then, on a day when crows freeze in midair, when tears gel on cheeks, when waterlogged limbs snap, Anna's temperature rises ten degrees. She pulls hair from her forehead and comes away with fingers salty with sweat. She realizes she hasn't gone to the bathroom for a long time. The dogs are not dogs. They are coyotes. Or wolves.

"There they go," said Diane.

"The boys," Dmitri said. "Off to races. All for you, understandably."

Thorbert and Christophe tore up a hill through the blizzard's veil. Dmitri arrived at the bottom to see them disappear.

"When did this country get so hilly?" Diane said.

"Thousand million years ago," said Dmitri, between heavy breaths. "Tectonics incident. A Tuesday morning, I think. Oldest mountains in the world, some say. Shortly after, organisms started to compete for space and energy."

"Wow. Ask a professor, get an answer. But funny you talk about competition for energy."

"Those two, anyway. Propelled by that most ancient impulse."

Diane Silverbow caught his arm as he stumbled towards a stump.

"Ill-fitted for our modern proportions."

Diane didn't know what the History Chair said half the time. His historic words sounded intelligent. And he was a Chair. He looked like a chair too, a comfortable recliner you could curl up inside. A man of ample mind, body, spirit.

The round man floated in a cloud of frosted flakes.

"We are not what we seem," he said. "Neither do we seem to be what we are."

The more she didn't understand him, the more Diane felt free. Tiny bells rang near her tympanic membrane, and a distant drum kept time. "It's funny," she said again, although her face was a placid receptacle, "that you should talk about energy."

"I have profound belief in energy. I simply do not possess it myself."

"Oh I don't think so."

She bent over. Dmitri thought: I am blessed to see this form of nature in the wilds. She unclipped her boots and fell backwards into the snow. This form of curves and circles in harmony with all around it. Powder exploded at her edges, then colonized nearby trees and her leather fringed coat. She traced her arms above her head, spread her legs and shut them. When she sat up they admired the form. A form one could curl around and keep safe.

"An angel," said Dmitri.

"An angel with a big butt," she said.

By the time they continued, it was almost buried.

The plan, she knows, is to run in the opposite direction until civilization returns, since Anna Hill is neither prepared to become a popsicle stand nor be licked at by wolves. But opposite is a relative notion.

The yelps of the beasts come from above, below, from underneath her skin. She flees from a random direction and maintains her course as the golden mean, then turns into the woods, which is when she sees the things twenty feet in front of her. The coyotes are surprised. The wind was right. Their attentions pinned on the sprawl of fur and blood at their feet.

The one nearest her turns and stares. Two others turn from the kill, but only long enough to give the fourth, the smallest, the quickest, time to snatch the remains and vanish into the pines. A second later the others tail it.

Anna realizes she has no breath. Then she is all breath. She runs. She's clear on opposite now. She has no concept otherwise of where, or how, she only moves. Her bootless wet foot is forgotten. She may have wet herself. Her body is hot. She has never been so in shape all her life. She tears off a scarf, lets it catch on the branches.

After ten minutes, Anna realizes she bounded across the whole clearing, across the slushy river and into the far woods. She holds her breath long enough to listen for the beasts, the sounds of sadistic German fairy tales: cackles, knives on stones, heavy breaths, guttural snarls. They won't look for her—they'll smell her out. Smell her fear, she's heard that. They'll smell her period. Turn their noses in the air and find her blood, the blood of the kill still on their lips. She doesn't look back. She doesn't feel her foot.

Where is everybody? The snow starts again, or maybe it's only wind redecorating the trees. It doesn't make it easier to find a trail. Civilization has abandoned her. She refuses to take off her glasses, no matter the frost on them. But everything has packed up and moved. Anna will spend her last minutes, perhaps her last hours, in the middle of nothing, pursued by beasts best left in children's books. She looks up in trees, tries to spot one that would shield and protect her, a benevolent spirit. She would take the assistance of Diane Silverbow now, would swallow whole her tales of Indigenous knowledge, of ten thousand years of harmony with the land, of the time she made her own snowshoes from birch bark and bulrushes. How did people *forget* someone? Was she that unremarkable?

A noise, and Anna drops her self-pity immediately. Nothing. She realizes she is hugging a tree. Lets it go. Grabs it again. Indistinguishable, the sound through the wind, the trees, her frozen ears. A school bus on a road, or a siren, or the comforting scream of an infant. The wind exhales and half of the tree above her shakes off the snow cradled in its branches. With a cry of shock and frustration, since much of the snow falls on her neck, Anna pushes the tree away from her. She trips on another tree prone underneath the snow, brings her head out of a snowdrift, wipes her eyes and looks up a rise to what must be a cabin, its chimney proud with smoke.

    She scrambles towards it. A half-forgotten trapper's outpost. She sees what looks like washtubs hung on the log walls, and as she gets closer, an enormous pair of antlers, elk or moose or mammoth. And over the door, mounted like bushman voodoo, a rusty axe.

    Her foot is frozen. That's good—she can feel it. But she's about to fling herself into a solitary shack, the last redoubt of some bearded misfit pushed to these limits for all his sins and heinous tics, who has not bathed or deloused his beard since last *St-Jean-Baptiste* and wouldn't he be delighted to have a half-dead Woman in Jeopardy knock on his door in the middle of a blizzard, all for himself to reinvigorate, and none of society's niceties to bother with.

    Her toes will drop off any minute now, one by one. Anna can do nothing but go forward. She is ready, she will stumble to that front door and claw her nails down its worn timber, and accept her fate. Except that with the next step a beast flies towards her. A thing of black fur. With fangs exposed. In approximately one second, it will land on top of her, and everything will go dark. In the first quarter second Anna shields her head. In another quarter second her lungs fill with frozen air and hold it. The rest of time is waiting.

"Sorry about Spencer," said the bushman. "He's starved for company."

The black-furred poodle sat at her feet now, satisfied to have licked her enough upon her arrival. Anna lay on the chaise-longue, wrapped in blankets and fur coats. The man handed her another cup of decaf chai tea, with honey he'd harvested himself. The ambulance was on its way, it just took a while to get here, he assured Anna. Everything took a while to get here. That's why they liked it, but it also led to insanity. I mean, they were here weekends, and longer in the summer, but his boyfriend (who'd forgotten to take his phone again and was in the village looking for half-way decent sashimi) did have concerns in Montreal, and one couldn't play at *nostalgie de la boue* all the time, it lost its flavour eventually. You know?

Anna didn't know, but she didn't much of anything, including feel her toes, or have conversational ideas, or taste how his honey tended more towards the woody than floral. She wasn't sure either whether they spoke French or English, or a private language they recently invented. He showed her how Spencer the poodle *attacked* his daily spoonful of honey, which helped his breath at least for a little while and had a list of benefits so long that Anna was unconscious before the end of it.

The urban bushman filled the emptiness between them with talk and fussed over her blankets and cooed noises for comfort, and when Anna was conscious she thanked him in numerous languages and felt her skin shiver with a life its own. If she tried to lift her head the shack would spin. But eventually she thought she felt better and she threw off her blankets and said she would walk from here, and take Katharine Hepburn with her for protection.

Immediately as she stood she fell over. The dog was thrilled to join her in the game, along with much barking and panting, mostly from his side. When the bushman got back into the room with more honey and tea he shrieked at her for getting out of the chaise. She was in no shape to do anything and he was sorry he had no car because Carl took far too long, and may have got distracted at the deli counter again, what with the new butcher and all. And he felt guilty, yes he could admit it out loud, that he hadn't stripped naked and her naked and cuddled for the body heat, but could you even imagine Carl's reaction, with a *woman*, and Spencer a spectator? At least he'd got her wet things off and in the dryer (sorry about the wool), and that was probably the ambulance now, picking its way down that unbladed road, or Carl, or at the worst some friends who said they *might* come, and they always said that but reneged at the last minute, and wouldn't that be hilarious if it was them now, in their Smart car? But the bushman didn't laugh, he sat in the chair across from her and put his face in his hands and sobbed as the flash of red lights filled the shack with alarm.

The phone rang every fifteen minutes. Mister Jackson Zaporzan had counted on a fine Sunday afternoon of televised sport, preferably the sweet science of boxing, interspersed with phases of sleep. But that insistent bell ruined everything. The phone wasn't even his. He heard it through the wailing wall that separated his Baronial castle from Anna's ersatz *château*, and pitied her phone's electronic crying jag. The sound echoed through Zap's undecorated rooms, bounced off his moving boxes, and drew him to his back balcony, where he tried to see in Anna's house. In case of an emergency. He couldn't see in her window. She'd been kidnapped. Zap leaned further into his balcony railing until it protested. Clipped on his tool belt. Hurried to Anna's front door. Jiggled it ajar. When he called up the stairs no one answered. The phone was silent. A few puffed rice cakes lay on the kitchen counter, so he helped himself, turned on the TV, and flipped through Anna's academic paper. He tore through the fridge for a drink after he almost choked.

When the phone rang on schedule, Zap assumed it was the kidnappers with the demand for ransom.

"Anna's house," he said through a mouthful of rice and white wine.

There was no sound. Zap was prepared to save Anna's life by either paying the ransom or preferably tracking down the bastards.

"Anna's husband here. What do you want?"

In the background the muffled bark of an impatient pug.

Zap held his breath. Still nothing. "I'm a retired policeman. Trained in sniffing trails."

Somebody let out a quick breath on the other end. "Sure you are. This is Anna's mother."

"Ah yes. I'm here to fix her door."

"Anna's not married, though."

"Not yet. But marriage is my ruse to throw the kidnappers off the trail."

"Kidnappers! Is Anna there?"

"Is that you rang all afternoon?"

"Otto, stop that. She always calls Sunday afternoons. If she doesn't come by. Sometimes we have tea, and sometimes she stays for supper. But she doesn't do that so much anymore."

Zap asked if they ate little sandwiches for tea, or leaned more toward sweets.

"Lately sweets. Does that mean something?"

"I see," Zap said, and nodded sagely, as he thought an investigator might do.

Dotty held the phone away when rice cake crunched in her ear. Her daughter ate on the phone all the time too. Always at least three tasks at once.

"Does she have any enemies ma'am?"

"I don't think she gets out enough for that."

Zap insisted that everything hinged on the door. If it closed properly, she would avoid this unwanted attention. Professors, with their high salaries and public lifestyle, were juicy targets for loonies.

"There was a French professor who took her to Paris." Dotty hadn't trusted that country since the Vichy government.

"Hm, hm," Zap said.

"He may have wanted to steal her research. They do that."

"Ha," Zap said. "The Frenchman doesn't present any danger as far as I know."

"How far do you know?"

"Not so far as I'd like."

"She doesn't answer her cell phone. I get an automatic message that she's not available."

"I get that too."

Dotty thanked him for his interest and it was a pleasure speaking to him and sorry to take him away from his door, but…

"Otto! Bad dog."

…would he be a dear and tell Anna to call her mother when she came home?

Zap was now part of the family. He tilted his head to one side. Married. He tilted it to the other side. Met the mother-in-law. Immediately his head drained of blood and floated ten inches above his body. He brought it down to his knees. The air was hot in Anna's house.

He should help out. Put away the rice cakes, although there was only one broken one left. Wipe the wine off Anna's paper. Get the toolbox. By the time he popped the doorknob off the phone rang again.

Zap's head shook.

Three seconds later someone thumped on the door.

"Nobody home," Zap said. "Go away." Through the doorknob hole nothing but a winter coat, dark blue, shell buttons. Did kidnappers dress like that? Did kidnappers make house calls for ransoms? Jehovah's Witnesses. And pamphlets.

"Put them through the hole."

"But this is the house of Professor Anna Hill?"

Quiet. Three fingers wriggled through the hole.

Zap whacked them with a wrench.

A string of Gallic curses followed, none of which blasphemed the church. The Frenchman.

The blue coat had backed away from the door. He cleared his throat. Zap saw his hands. They held no pamphlets, but the one that rubbed the injured fingers held an envelope. The Frenchman backed away till Zap could see his face. Couldn't see his eyes behind the sunglasses. The man smoothed his hair and looked down at the steps.

"We thought it better," he tried again, "at the history department." Christophe bent down to look through the hole, but kept his distance. The door stayed pushed shut from inside. Tiny attempts at thaw dripped from the roof above.

Christophe let out a short laugh. "It has weighed on us. I have hardly eaten since then." Inside his pocket was a depleted packet of French antacid tablets. "At least not anything of worth."

Zap took his hand off the door. He watched it swing open an inch. Not properly balanced. More problems.

Christophe put the fingers of his good hand on the edge of the door to push it open. "We completed our ski trip before Anna resurfaced."

The door slammed shut, but this time Christophe pulled his fingers out in time. A single drop of melted snow fell on his head. Christophe ran his hand through his hair again, left a grey tuft sticking in the air.

"I am a professional colleague."

"Good for you. I'm Anna's husband."

Zap watched Christophe back away from the door, lean against the railing, cross his arms.

"I'm sure you are. Although since she is not currently married, you are the handyman, at best."

Zap didn't answer, but gripped his wrench tighter.

"So I will leave this here. I drew up a list of Anna's ski errors, in the hope that she could benefit from her mistakes. In point form." He began to push the curled envelope through the door knob hole. Zap, who deemed that it could well be a list of ransom demands, pushed it back.

For a while they competed over the envelope, until finally Christophe tore it out, turned around and started down the stairs to the street. On the sidewalk he stopped and fished for an antacid tablet. This city was filled with Barbarians.

"The thing with doors," Zap said, "is that they think themselves perfect, but are in fact as sensitive as old queens in winter castles." He wanted to add more, about the latch alignment, and loose hinges, and re-drilling holes with a three-eighths bit, but Christophe was on his way back up and Zap slammed the door shut again. He peered through the hole. "No more love notes," Zap said.

The door flew open towards him after Christophe kicked it in, and would have made a bloody mess of his face had there been a doorknob. As it was Zap's nose fit into the hole, and his wide forehead absorbed most of the blow. Still, the hit knocked him spread-eagled on his ass, unleashed a cartoon flock of benign birds that circled above him, and left him squinting into a Sunday afternoon sun partially eclipsed by a massive and well-coiffed planet of a head.

The planet yelled and pointed. Zap looked up at the flaring nostrils and teeth and finger pointed down at him and tried to make sense of the words. "What have you done to...where in your *putain* Montreal apartment..." The face grew red as Mars, the feet kicked at everything in their way, including Zap's legs, his toolbox, the doorknob. "I have confronted doors with hardware hundreds of years older than this... I have battled men and women who hold more power than you can fathom... divine vengeance... Blaaam! ... insolence, what shame...." Or something like that—Zap had to translate quickly, and with the disadvantage of a slight concussion. In his other hand, he realized, he held a sanding block to ward off any more blows.

The phone rang again. Zap used the interruption to run up the stairs.

"Oh, I'm glad I got you," Dotty said.

"Hey Mom," Zap said.

Christophe came up the stairs. He took another tablet from his pocket.

"It's Zaporzan. Jackson is my..."

Dotty was out of breath. Her daughter, she confessed, got into unusual situations ever since childhood, even though they—Anna's father included, at least until the Great Blizzard of nineteen ninety-three—had done all they could to remove external stimuli.

"Oh yeah."

Christophe had found the last rice cake. He crunched near the phone, his sunglasses still on.

But they had tried, Dotty said, to direct her towards the safety of being a teacher, which meant she had to read a lot of books. But that apparently safe outlet led to more unusual situations, and… What she wanted to say was, thank you. At least somebody took care to shim up her daughter's frail home.

Anna's apartment swirled when Zap closed his eyes. When he held his forehead his fingers came away with blood.

Dotty let out a long breath. Anna had called, and she was waiting at the emergency room at the hospital but she wasn't kidnapped or on her deathbed or anything of the sort.

"She's all right," Zap said, and touched Christophe's shoulder. The Frenchman jolted backwards and was gone.

"Although there might," Dotty said, "be some toenail issues."

8. Stranded With A Stranger

Her proud protestations were birdsong. The cowboy wrestled her girdled waist. His paws peeled her off the mud road and slung her behind the saddle. Their fate was inevitable: she cursed and snubbed all help, and he was the last law in the runaway mine town. Anyone could see transformation coming like the cavalry. The train would make its run, and the abused miners get their payday, and the bandits their tombstones. Yup, that's how life would be from now on little lady, you got black and you got white, and you better learn 'em now. That's how life was each time this old Western played on Anna's TV.

Anna's feet floated on a pillow on the coffee table beside a cloud of lemon ginger herbal tea, and she feared for her life as she'd known it. She kept lists. Schedules were posted on her walls, her weekly planner was lifeblood, but she'd never thought of herself as a slave to routine. She'd once been called a free spirit (by a scientific boy who ran from her interest in anatomy experiments). But now the inability to get up and go to the bookshelf without a thousand needles piercing her toes was enough to revolutionize her life.

Not only did her handicap rob her of necessary habits, it also forced her to face all the inadequacies sprinkled through her papers. And the more her toes blackened, the closer the monstrous deadline for the *Journal of Medieval Torture and Academic Suicide* staggered.

That date—that beast—attacked her paper, ripped open her reason and exposed her conjecture. On her couch she wielded a yellow pen to highlight each mistake and failure.

As a student, if she couldn't craft a proper paper she only feared a flunk and a second run at the class. Now there were few chances of do-overs. She could miss her one shot at a professorship and then look at twenty wasted years behind her. When one started to meander down that path of self-doubt it wasn't deadlines but all manner of little demons that popped out of the hedges. A nasty one nagged about the loss of her house if she couldn't meet the mortgage. An identical hideous twin whispered about the inevitable little death when she would have to move back to her mother's house. But she could not ignore the mammoth in the room: the next twenty years alone and with enough time to stare at the result of her inability to love. Might as well begin now. Anna began to relive each thing she said and did with Christophe in the woods, and mark them in her mind with yellow, until the grey day was filled with dyed streaks of fluorescent sunshine.

Anna limped to the window to see if there was any real sunshine. There wasn't. But it was something to do. She pulled her bathrobe high around her neck when she saw the snow. A few stray students navigated the sidewalks. She began a game: if she saw a woman alone she would get to work on her paper. A man alone, and she imagined him on his way to see her for a secret rendezvous. A couple… there were no couples. Anna relaxed her hold on the bathrobe around her neck. All lovers were inside the houses down the block, warming each other against the winter's breath. Her toes burned.

Anna pressed a button and the new sheriff and his western world went mute. She pried open the maw of her laptop.

Yet neither completely exhaustive nor authoritative is the Tawq-al-hamamah, the "Ring of the Dove," the tenth-century Arab treatise on transcendence that masquerades, perhaps even to its educated composer, as a manual on love. The seemingly incongruent pleasures of the flesh here are first secret, then adulterous, and ultimately inspirational.

Behind the computer screen a cowboy stumbled through an Arizona landscape of dust and sand. A close-up of leather chaps, his hand brushed them clean. His chin unshaven, his mouth breathing in the hot air. That's what Coleridge Park needed, a square-jawed sheriff to round up students, keep the streets free of snide French professors, grab Anna by the waist and put her on the right track. She felt her neck and shivered, though her skin was warm under the robe.

The heroes of the desert romances are normatively the poets themselves, which may explain, without the exclusion of other motivations, the tendency towards abstraction and away from earthly motivations.

Earlier, after her bath, she'd turned up the heat in the living room. Now the sun prepared to slip behind Mount Royal for its late afternoon siesta, a last glimmer atop the trees. A pair of dark eyes on the TV, with a bead of sweat between them. Unflinching eyebrows. The cowboy writhed through the dust on his belly.

In the sources, the romance poets of the Occitane who followed inevitably used the construction of love as *solace*; yet a reading of both interpretations reveals that in both cultures the poets "omitted the final solace" not out of a sense of shame or awkward prudishness for the sexual act, but instead out of an inflated respect for a pure communion, a spiritual lust.

She couldn't do it. The sun glared at her and she couldn't see the screen for a second, nor the TV. The only thing she needed was that grant to research in Spain, and with it, tenure. Her hand shielded her eyes, and she let it glide over her eyelashes, her nose, her lips. Tenure, and someone to come home with. She sank deeper and pulled a cloud blanket off the back of the sofa, fluffed it over her feet. Anna placed the laptop on her legs. That, and a transporting love. She paused the cowboy as he lifted his head, and opened a blank file.

A patch of sky could be glimpsed intermittently through the moving clouds…and from it a shaft of golden Spanish sun filtered down through the dust, seemingly guiding a lone figure on horseback along the narrow spine of a hilltop. A piercing shriek, followed by what may have been a laugh, entered the shaft of light, seeming to break it apart. Something dark circled above the ridge, something feathered and beaked. The falcon could see over the next hill, still four times as high as the tallest spire in the complex. The falcon, who could spot the twitch of a mouse from that height, saw no movement in the courtyard. At mid-afternoon in the Kingdom of León, it was hardly unusual.

The man on horseback, his tattered robes and scarves still now in the breezeless expanse, stopped and raised a hand above his eyes against the harsh Spanish sun. He followed the movements of the bird—knew its motions so well as to converse with the beast yet a mile away. And the bird said: all is quiet, all you seek are sleeping, or dead.

Chilled, the falconer continued on, his saluki sniffing out the more earthly concerns. Then the dog stopped, and the man heard what the dog heard too. A collective moan from the dry sands; the whole nunnery full, chanting our morning matins, accented by the desperate cries of a pack of wolves.

I, Angeles the nun, knew before anyone else of the imminent arrival of the Morisco Falconer.

Anna looked up. Darkness had crept into the room. The cowboy was frozen in place on the TV. The paragraphs took an hour at least. She'd hit a literary black hole. Couldn't remember anything. Had been *there* in the desert with the Falconer, had put her in first person. She peeled back her blanket and touched the sheen of perspiration on her stomach. She traced it around her belly button, underneath her pyjamas. Her hand fell between her legs. She was wet. Anna looked around, in case any cowboys or falconers watched. They didn't. She slid her fingers inside. Her lips parted, breathed in the hot air.

Images flashed through her mind too fast. Her breaths came faster and turned into whispers, and the whispers into incantations. At the murky edges of pleasure another voice joined her, then a chorus of gunshots. She bolted upright, pulled the blanket to her chin. She'd hit the television remote. The gunslinger had come to life, evaded attack, and given way to a commercial. A family sang the praises of soap.

She stared at the images, her mouth agape. Let out a breath. Her legs were weak, both from the surprise and from stretching them hard to the floor. Her toes burned more than ever. She fell back again, swallowed. The computer screen cast a blue light on the coffee table.

Anna smiled. One day of enforced vacation and she turned into a hedonist. Her work morphed into fantasy and her fantasies to sex. She didn't move from beneath the comforter. Maybe unhealthy. Back at the University, did everyone know she was incapacitated on this couch, that she avoided work, got too excited about old movies, wrote romances? She'd be excommunicated by the Inquisitors. And what kind of role model was she for Audrey? A young, easily influenced... Anna flipped off the blanket and stood up. She had to text Audrey now. She hadn't arranged for her class tomorrow. Either cancel or give an assignment or Audrey would take it. On her way to find her phone Anna bumped her toes and crumpled into a simpering mess.

Audrey calmed her with a reply, told her to rest, everything was taken care of. She and Dmitri had arranged a guest speaker. Wonderful, Anna replied. So easily replaced. Nice to feel indispensable. But it did calm her, because after only two days she was so far from the University that when she looked out her window she expected to see another city on the horizon, or two moons rising, or a vast and barren expanse of desert stretching from Coleridge Park to the black sky.

A Morisco Falconer. Now she was sure, the Romance hero would be Morisco not Moor, a blend of the two cultures, so much more intrigue to it, and representative of the rivalry and bitter... No. The appearance of Moriscos, Muslims who publicly converted to Catholicism for safety reasons, would put the story somewhere in the early 1500s, specifically Charles the I's decree in 1512. But that would be a little late; perhaps an earlier unrepentant Moor in around 1000 when Alfonso pushed the kingdom of Léon past Salamanca, or even earlier when Ramiro "the Devil" made a no-man's land of the Rio Duero that separated Christian and Muslim.... Anna stopped herself. What had the woman on the plane said? Keep your history on a leash. And clean up after it.

> The nunnery's fountain tiles were dry. No rain had fallen for two years. Our nuns' habits were the colour of dust, and our vile

bodies, and probably our insides too. Every morning as I went to the garden of herbs I looked to the heavens and demanded mercy and rain and none came.

Except this morning. This morning, the Lord answered me. In the form of a falcon, spinning a wheel of fortune over the women. I watched it. Its rhythm made me dizzy. I knelt in the middle of the courtyard.

That was how the Mother found me. For the Abbess was hurrying to the massive wooden door that shut us all away from the world. Outside, out there, a stranger was beset by demons.

A little thick-fingered on the dry fountains, but what do you want? This wasn't a doctoral thesis. Not that at all. She popped two more painkillers.

They ran in madness about a thing only half alive. The Abbess and I stood frozen at the portico. One of the wolves lunged within the circle and emerged with a bloody snout, and an animal whimper rose in the still air. Another looked up, saw two more victims, and bounded towards us.

A sabre came whistling past my head, and with perfect aplomb cut the wolf in his neck. Immediately it crumpled to the ground, and the rest of the wolves scattered in the wind.

In the sand kneeling was a Moor, his robes half ripped from him, his chest not hiding a fresh long scar. His turban had come loose in the fight, and I saw his hair night black, glossy and falling over his thick shoulders. His gaze fell on me without censure, and the Abbess instinctively grabbed me and pulled me into her robes. I wanted to stay there, shivering against the danger I'd only just escaped. But I couldn't breathe and pushed away the Mother, and from out of the sky like an arrow the falcon descended with a shriek; its talons out like swords and wings spread like an avenging angel. I watched it land on the Moor's outstretched arm. My insides tightened. My fear mixed with a world of feelings I'd never had before, feelings that began in my heart and ended between my legs. I no longer wanted to be the bride of Christ. I wanted to be the Moor's falcon.

She could *touch* him. There he was. The desert odor of his skin and the scratch of his beard. Anna looked up from her computer, realized she felt the same way the nun did. Pushed her chair from the desk. She could feel him more than she had in years of exegesis on the attire and habits and religion of the Moors. The wolves were to blame. The coyotes, their teeth in the rabbit, the blood on their lips. Anna wiggled her toes. And the dog of course, the one that leaped on her as she crawled from the wilderness. In its excitement to see a visitor it had nipped her lip, and she tasted her own blood. Was it like they said, a beast that has tasted blood…well she had tasted the Moor's blood, she'd tasted the outer limits of death. And speaking of which, had she taken those painkillers yet? She took two more.

Anna eased her feet onto her desk. He wanted her. But she didn't give herself away like that. She was in control. It was time for some context.

> In the new millennium of anno Domini 1000 when the Moors had entered the land as liberators, brought life to the dry peninsula and irrigated it with their knowledge, sprouting jewels of palaces and gardens and verdant growths of maths and sciences, tolerating the religions of the other People of the Book, and bringing to Europe their paper and salt and silk and satin and pepper and clocks and soaps and maps and globes and furs,

Rahman III sat in Cordoba amid his library of four hundred thousand books and wept for...

But who wanted to be in control? The Moor wasn't seduced by her education.

The Moor's heart longed for the hospitallers and libraries of Cordoba; the books that spread out all the information for surgeons; their beliefs in tiny "contagious entities" entering the body during the Plague, while the Europeans still mumbled incantations and foraged among...

Easy there, girl. Let the story go.

His robes were ragged; his horse more so. The trek took him across a wild, untamed plain filled with bandits and beasts and barbaric Christians, his robe still wet with rainwater, clinging to his chest and biceps. He shook himself like a wild thing, then let his mount carry him on. That trek of danger meant two days of fatal risk; today it can be crossed in ten minutes by car.

You couldn't do that, of course. Although if she did it right, maybe she could innovate. Put in a footnote.

But what could be done, Anna thought, what should be done, is that she didn't need the Moor to come rescue everyone. Those that dressed like Moors seemed incompetent in search and rescue, and women were left to rescue themselves, and did fine thank you. Now was the time of the Other Gender.

When I saw the pack of demons I drew my fingers between my breasts and then from nipple to hard nipple and sang *Creator Spirit, Come*, with my arms raised up, and *Send Forth Thy Spirit* and slowly drew off one by one my garments and crosses of my Lord, and I cried "Thou who didst condescend to be born of a

Virgin, have mercy on us!" until I was almost naked and open before him. "Oh Lord, open thou my lips," I pleaded, I rubbed the sign of the cross all over me, consumed by the fire that took all the air from the parched desert.

Mercy. I could not let the Moor see me further, nor let my heart free. The saints cried, "The heart is a full wild animal!" Cloistered in the abbey I kept my eyes from seeing, my young complexion shut away from the sun and Spanish men. And I didn't think any more of him, and instead tried to do as the Abbess instructed, to turn my thoughts to the pain that prisoners endured, lying in fetters of iron, of Christians in the dungeons of the heathen. But I was bound like them, and I lay with them, I lay with the Moor amid the chains and dust and despair.

Anna went to take a shower.

She sat on a stool and kept her precious toes from the needles of water. The hot water ran through her red hair and over her face and she sat trying not to think or feel. But it took concentration, and her face was scrunched up with effort, and her shoulders tight, and sometimes she forgot her toes and brought them under the shower and screamed at herself. Then she thought about why she tried not to think, and thought maybe because she was doodling around with a stupid fantasy when she should instead finish her papers. The shower began to hurt more than just her toes. Like her whole body had frozen and only now began to wake.

That nun and Moor stuff was over the top. But she recognized those last paragraphs as the medieval Nun's Rule, patched together from undergrad days. Was it plagiarism if the text was eight hundred years old? And who would read it anyway? Who would mouth the words, caress the pages, fall under the spell she put on them every night?

The Abbess pushed three of us toward the Moor, and we grabbed his arms, knotted and warm, and pulled him through the gate leaving a trail, dark and wet. He was covered in blood and sweat, and he struggled to keep his eyes open. His hand searched me out, gripped on my torn robe like a holy relic. When his head fell back his gaze penetrated deep inside me.

I was brought back by the cries of the Abbess shouting for balms, for lettuces and spices and opium. She commanded me to fetch water—as if it lay all about in abundance. I found enough, a bowl I was careful not to let spill. His robes were pulled to the side, his tunic pulled to the waist. The abbess took the water and poured it over his darkened chest. We gasped and stepped back. A gash from a sword or knife split his flesh.

This was Julia's fault: her rhapsody on the wounded alpha male. Made Anna go all romantic poet in the shower, everything wet and slippery and scrubbed. And then right there, with melted toes and careless heart, Anna understood that under the influence of Angeles, the Moor was the first romance poet. Not some inky dreamer. He was the first to bring that veiled fire to the Christians, for them to ignite their troubadours. She hobbled back to her laptop in a towel.

The Moor came into my life like a hunter in the raw desert. I was drawn to him unlike anything ever before. Maybe it was hypnotism—we didn't know the secret powers of the dark men from the south. He was wounded, but I was wounded too, not with scars you could see, but he saw, he had more than one scar. We reflected each other. His hunting, his weapons were my balm, even as I prayed they would not kill the both of us. Later I would find his poetry: "The gazelle stumbled in the hunt and showed the side of her heart. She looked into my eyes and became the hunter with me. My arrows stayed in their quiver, for I could not wound her."

It was lucky his horse had followed the sheep-drove path to the isolated cloister. Not only because he was a Moor in Christian territory, and might find a hint of mercy here. But that wound would need divine intervention. The alignment of stars. My tears fell on his wounds and seared his heart.

"He will die," the Abbess said.

She looked at me. "It was you who saved him from the wolves. They scattered from your prayers." The Mother looked at the heavens. The other nuns looked up as well, then to me. Not all the eyes were admiring. "Angeles, you will tend him until then. At the least we can comfort him until he meets his god." I licked my fingers. They tasted of blood and disaster, desire and pain. His good hand reached up again to me, brushed my breasts, held my arm, pulled me down to him. A breath, a garbled marriage of Arab and Christian tongues came out of his thick lips.

I understood nothing. I understood everything. I didn't want any more those passionate prayers to a stone figure. I wanted to kneel before this Moor, this man, and search through his tunic, to find him hard for me, to fall back and sweat and moan and let no gods stop me from being as rough as he, to command and be listened to, even as he held me down, his mouth wet, his dark eyes fierce, his black hair whipping my...

"Hello?" Anna answered the phone on the first ring.

"Have you tried cayenne pepper?"

She was guilty, she was caught, she wanted rescue. All she needed was Christophe's voice. But she got her mother.

When she was excited Dotty forgot formalities like *Hello*. Anna said she couldn't talk because she was in the middle of her paper for the *Journal of Medieval Misbehaviour.* Her mother said you didn't answer the phone if you couldn't talk.

"Because they say it can do both in one shot."

"Who says what?"

"Sprinkle it on your toes, that gets the blood circulation alive. They do it in China for frostbite."

"Mom, in China they think Canadian seal penises are aphrodisiacs."

"And if you put it on the dog bite it helps sweat out the dog saliva."

"The penis?"

"I swear Anna, you only want to say that word."

Dotty wondered out loud about a tetanus shot, since it sounded like the beast had been out of control, even though Anna had already informed her it was a poodle, and the wound more an errant scratch, and the hunter's shack a sort of Bed and Breakfast, with decaf chai. But then her mother didn't understand much of Anna's world. That whole episode with the neighbour who had fixed her door, for instance. Encouraged by Dotty. "I feel better Mom, thanks. Like I said, I'm at work on my paper." Anna sent the Moor to her printer to provide appropriate busy noises.

"Can you put on your makeup?"

This was the mother she understood.

"Trauma, honey. You don't know how it affects you till it's too late."

"Thanks. I'll put on makeup. If I ever go outside again."

"Anyway, when you can, Auntie Pearl wants you to come to her complex and invite her here for Christmas dinner."

Anna paused to figure out what her mother meant. "Well right now my toes are ready to fall off."

"She's all alone and she knows too what it's like to not have a body part. Can you do that for her? You've got a few weeks off school? You don't have any boys come by anymore."

They were still boys to Dotty.

Anna left the Moor alone with his spices. She had been prepared to wash his hair in cinnamon and licorice and cumin, to sprinkle rose petals or lavender in the nun's bath, to have everyone in the romance in bloom like springtime in goddamn Provence. But her toes were the Black Death.

> There was only one way out, and it was to remember the kiss of peace in the mass. And so I forgot all the world and rose out of my body, and embraced my beloved who went down on me from heaven, into my breast's bower. I held him fast until he granted whatever I wished, tightly clasping God's rood, and I fell before the tracks of wolves half afaint, and tried to do as the Abbess instructed, to neither do any thing, nor think, any thing.

9. Checkmate

Christophe sashays into the classroom, a sultan in a cold harem. They're undergrads. They think of themselves, they think of nothing. So simple to be five moves ahead of everyone else. He's taken Anna's pawns and he's not satisfied. He will be more than a visitor, he will be a Chair, he will be a Dean, he will show this outpost what power and knowledge is. The university back in Paris will understand they lost more than a professor when they sent him to Winterville. Without preamble he projects an image of a medieval hand mirror. "The game is everywhere," Christophe says, stepping down from the lectern. "And not only a man's game. Impressed on everything a lady might hold in her hand." He stops at Audrey's desk, picks up her phone, studies its back as if fixing his hair in the reflection. "Carved in ivory in her hand mirror, on her combs, the same on her casket. And you will love this, you undergraduates, with your thrill of symbol and innuendo. Does our lady study the art of war?"

The students look up from their phones and laptops and minds. Are they supposed to answer that? Why a chess game? Wasn't Professor Anna Hill's class supposed to reflect the role of the spice trade in the flavour of intimate medieval relations?

Christophe puts his hands on Audrey's desk front and centre and fixes his eyes on hers. Someday he will be Principal and

Chancellor here, and Paris will burn. "Will it be war, milady? Or but a simple *passe-temps*?"

"It can't be war," Audrey says. "No woman was even considered for battle."

Christophe doesn't take his eyes off her and hears nothing but the reflection of his own voice. The girl's bones shiver and she grins but doesn't look away. He tosses the phone back on her desk. A selfie of him appears on the other side now. She moves her hands away. "What is it?" he asks her. The other students can't look away either. "What do you play at?"

The girl's lips flutter. They are thick and painted and she licks one corner.

"Pardon?"

"Love," the girl says. Her head down, her eyes slide up to Christophe's eyes.

"Love!" He slams her desk, and the phone slides off into her lap. "Image number three!" His immaculate scarf follows the sweep of his arm, and another image shows a young man and woman playing chess in a tent, nothing untoward about that, carved in ivory and laid in state at the Louvre. But Christophe runs to the screen, puts both hands on the image, first caresses the draperies gouged out of tusk, then turns his back on it to shield it from the students' eyes. "Sex and violence," he says, "the Hollywood of the day: conflict and unbearable tension. All these are here, and even the arsenal for the game at hand: all is arranged beforehand, there are moves you must make and others forbidden. Oh, it is chaste, wanton and chaste, they don't touch or even meet eyes—" Here he glances back at Audrey in the front row, who has not yet looked elsewhere, and he toys with his ring — "but it appears that he has achieved checkmate." He looks around for something, spots an umbrella of Anna's in a dusty corner and uses it as his pointer. And without ever a move too brusque, in full command of the students' attention, the French professor points to where the man grasps the tent pole like his lance, and to the soft lines of the lady, her robes like buttercream in folds of velvet cloth, and to her sex—at his pronunciation of the word some in the class draw in their breath—and everywhere the curtains and the clothes and the tent all combine to announce (he takes a well-timed breath himself here, prepares to put his heart and umbrella thrust into the six syllables) her *pénétrabilité*.

"Well," says Audrey the next day on the phone, "I mean he did engage the class, you have to give him that."

"Buttercream?"

"It wasn't in your syllabus." Anna didn't respond for a while. "I am sorry I missed it. So he volunteered to step in."

"Till you're on your toes, in his words. I audit the class now. Since my incident with the classroom door."

Telephone lines rattled in the wind.

"Do you need me to come by?" Audrey said. She hoped Anna's moodiness was a side effect of her medication.

More silence, then a sigh.

"Too much history," Anna said.

"Anyway, if I come you could help me with the direction of my thesis," said Audrey, who was not at all concerned with her work, although Anna's last statement did sound like a good thesis title.

"Maybe I have too many classes... sometimes I...."

"I know. Never as straightforward as we'd like," Audrey interrupted. She had to get over there now, with a bottle of wine, otherwise she'd lose her impressionable advisor. "I'm using that

Mimesis quote in the thesis: 'The historical comprises a great number of contradictory motives in each individual, a hesitation and ambiguous groping on the part of groups.'"

Anna had only been away from the University a few days and already her head felt liberated from the mother country. In the world of the FalconMoor, she was sure that the motives and groping would all be straightforward.

Part II:
Hot Bacon

And at the heart of it all,
The lure that makes war an addiction for some people —
That hot bacon smell of pure contradiction.
— Anne Carson, *The Beauty of the Husband*

10. The Risky Journey Bath

"You place the unbaked chapatti over the dog bite," Sanjay says, bent halfway over the counter. He watches the curtains over his shoulder. "Leave it for fifteen minutes."

"It's not so much the dog bite," Anna says. "I think he only managed to scratch me with his claws. The frostbite on the other hand…"

"Then, peel off the chapatti and offer it to another dog. This is the moment. If he disdains it, you were attacked by a mad dog."

Sanjay shows more interest in Anna's wilderness injuries than anyone else. No one has taken responsibility. Not even Anna. Until she gets an apology from someone, anyone, she will pretend they don't exist.

"How is the short story Sanjay?" Anna cradles her bottle of Sunlight detergent. The only way to get him off that track is to discuss their mutual difficulty with words. She hasn't told anyone except Julia about her future as a best-selling romance novelist.

Anna cooks for one, but the dishes have an invasive root system. The ground must be cleaned before growth. Everything must be in order. When things are unresolved she sits down to write and fails.

Deeply nested in her computer lies the late article on *Illuminating Embodied Qualities of Gender in Cathar Medieval Erotics* for the *Journal of Medieval Nitpickers*, unseen, unmodified, unerotic. Within lie cocoons of research with folded wings. They chew on wit. They feed on irony. They make claims about socially unintelligible gender and the inherent instability of romance in the material-semiotic realm. They unpack performativity in the historic irony of marriage, of heteronormative performance in the Marxist model, of tragic liminalativity and gendercoloniality. They are so weighted they will not fly.

"The short story evolves," Sanjay says. "You have heard of Flash Fiction? So. I thought of you today. Yes I did. I read the newspaper. Research for my story."

Anna looks at the front door of her house. There is no line up of people bringing casseroles and wool slippers.

"It was in the Wanted Men and Women. Here it is." Sanjay pulls a torn piece of newspaper from under the twenty-dollar bills.

"'I need a specialty man,'" he reads. "'Awfully intelligent, yet able to enjoy simple pleasures like TV and vegetable chips.' Those are not so good for you as you think," Sanjay says. "I continue. 'He should look like Nikola Tesla and have the grace and manners of Cary Grant, but not know it. He should be strong…'"

There are mumbles from the back room.

"'…but never use his strength against me. He should protect me and let me be free. He should never leave, and never have been left himself. He should cry and show his vulnerability but have the determination of El Cid.'"

"That girl wants it all," Anna says. "But I only need this Sunlight."

"Miss Hill, this is not you who wrote this, with reference to Spanish heroes? Because this specialty man—this man that you write of, Miss Hill: is me."

When your local depanneur owner knows about your Man Trouble, thinks Anna, when he picks out Wanted men like horoscopes… Sanjay beams, his gapped teeth shine.

"You and I," Sanjay begins, his hand fathering her shoulder. Anna hears clucks behind a curtain in the back room, spies the flash of a yellow plastic butterfly hair clip. "You and I, we are writers. We understand."

"Good night Sanjay."

"These historical men you pursue. These knights in sparkled armour. El Cid the Kid. The bad boy you edit to a good man."

The bell tinkles as Anna leaves.

"Don't forget the chapatti," Sanjay says. He follows her to the door and hands her a bag of them. "Go get your man," he calls out into the snowflakes. "Your great Northman hero!"

Anna walks up her stairs alone.

And hungry. Too long at the hairdressers with her head in the sink, her toes in the air. The shampooer sculpted and the receptionist hurried a decaf espresso, clients murmured and hair dryers blew siroccos through fountains of youth. Women lay like recently retired caryatids, stone hair loosed and restored by conservationists.

Anna does her best work at the hairdresser. She pays people to fuss over her. Then her brain unlocks, all theory and abstraction and hypothesis. Would Christophe respect her as a brunette? Does her red hair stand for moral degeneration and witchery, or does it give her more of the Virgin Queen vibe, fierce and fit to conquer the world? Should she straighten her hair like that impossible slim girl beside her? Her romance nun did nothing, but remained irresistible to men. Not like these women in stages of disassembly. Makeovers were not for history professors. The stylist gasped and pointed to the woman in the mirror: What hair! Tamed and framed, Anna said. She left a huge tip.

At her door she peeks at the neighbour's house to make sure he isn't spying on her. She backs down a few steps to see if he's in the front window. Checks her door and mail slot for grand apologies, confessions, assurances. Nothing. Her fingers find the icy key. She locks the cold out.

"Anna."

A man's voice, top of the stairs. She doesn't breathe. A strange timbre.

"How must I spend these hours without you."

She should know this voice.

"All day you are at the baths."

"The baths? I got my hair done." Her voice is too high.

"Let me see you, creature of the North." His gaze envelops her, despite her resistance. She loves the bad boys.

Anna does not panic. Only a few days ago she came home to find the Moor waiting. She washed his feet of the desert. Everything went well until the Mother Superior started to worry about Plague and infection. He disappeared soon after, and Anna cut the Plague out. The story was a romance, for god's sake. But this is not the Moor. Three things disconcert:

1. The man's costume, or lack of it; he chose Anna's over-loved housecoat to wrap himself in;
2. The evidence that even though he is short, big-headed and wears a sword, the housecoat fits him better than it does her;
3. He is Attila the Hun, and he smells of battle.

"I have lit the fire. Come lay your body next to mine. You shiver."

Her coat falls to the floor. The fireplace has permanent plastic logs. Attila the Hun wipes the drippings of barbecued horseflesh from his beard. The smoke in the apartment isn't too heavy, and bends the light into puzzles reminiscent of a bazaar. From a far alleyway, a musician's lament drifts through her windows. Anna collapses on the couch and her plastic shopping bag spills out Sunlight.

"This place is a refugee camp," she says.

A horde of clothing and footwear invades the chairs and handles and corners of her house. Dishes and leftovers totter on the kitchen counter. He entertained his generals here. But they are gone now. He alone remains, a wild beast with facial scars. A retired rock star in eye shadow. When she wants to put her feet on her coffee table, she sees he has busted it up to roast his lunch in the middle of the living room.

He pulls her off the couch. Although he is more sedentary these days and prefers to rule with his head, not his hand, his grip still overwhelms.

"I cannot leave without you. I would come to steal you away." He unbuttons her blouse, brushes cut hair from her shoulders. Rough hands tickle. "Why do you pursue education when you have me? All day I sit here, think of nothing but how lucky your students are to study your lips as they form multisyllabic buzzwords." Attila bends to her neck, breathes hot breath of lust on her throat.

"Post-intentional," Anna murmurs. "Unessentialistic. LGBTIQQIAAP. Heteronormatively Transandrogynous."

Playing house with Attila isn't easy. But he knows what he wants. And what he wants, other than Western Europe, is her. He plans ambushes on her vulnerability with maps and diagrams and counselors. He outlines the fortresses he will build for her nestled along the banks of the Rhine. Anna's toes tingle. He is a man obsessed. In the past she would have labeled that as emotional instability, but in him—he pulls her atop him now with the same ease and familiarity with which he saddles a horse—in him it is strength. And the way he clasps her waist, floating her… some would try to convince her that protectiveness was control and abuse. His voice rumbles in her ear, demands marriage and a son for his Empire. He promises escapes to Constantinople and Budapest, shopping excursions in Rome and Paris. But they come from such different places—she, Montreal's West Island, he, a boiling river of blood in Dante's seventh circle of hell.

Afterwards, sprawled and breathless, Anna wonders if she could dress him among the shops of Paris. Attila in her housecoat, bone in one hand and pitcher of wine in the other. Could she tame him, tease out the tortured boy? Wasn't he a romantic at heart? Hadn't he accidentally founded Venice when people fled to the lagoon islands to escape his sword?

"Look what I have discovered." Attila turns on the radio. "It is a blast from the past." Squeaky voices from Motown pour from the speakers, claiming love is as easy as one, two, three.

He can move. Anna jumps up from the bed to join him. She shakes her hair and jiggles her hips until they laugh on the rug.

"Hunny," Anna says, "maybe we should take a bath."

By Hunnic standards it is an extravagance, but Attila is fascinated by Anna's customs. Now bubbles explode through his chest hair, water steams from pipes on command, and an array of candles softens Anna's complexion. The heat forces her to open a window and shiver at the cool air on her skin. She holds out a white cake. He bites.

"Wait, wait," Anna says, "You clean yourself with it."

Attila takes another bite.

She wants to ask him so many questions: Do you care about me? Am I a fling? Why didn't you lay waste to Rome? But whenever she tries to reach out, he retreats.

"Then, when we are dry," Attila says, "you will lie with me again."

"Maybe you'd like to shave."

"When we are born," he says, "our cheeks are burned with a hot iron. We shave but once. And we are bathed by the gods when it rains."

He reaches for her thigh. Wind blows cold through the open window. His fingers slide to her knee, over and underneath, then down her calf to her foot. Anna exhales slowly so nothing will change.

"I would plunder no more, for this. They can keep the treasures of Rome."

"Maybe a few trinkets?"

The cathedral bells of Anna's cell phone launch into a jubilant chorus. The lovers ignore the noise and believe the angels rejoice, though Anna does let out a relieved sigh when they stop. She remakes her vow to always leave it on vibrate. Ten seconds later, as her lips part for his, her doorbell chimes in distinct ecclesiastical tones.

"Oh dear," she says. More historical suitors lined up at her door. She'd have to tell them.

"I'm already seeing someone," she'd say.

"Who?"

"The Scourge of God. You'd better go."

The door chimes ring again. She knows who it is. The neighbour. All the better. She would send Attila to answer. And that damn carpenter would blurt a kafuffle of blather, lean on the door frame and try a sardonic leer. Attila in that open robe nursing a Sambuca. He'd go crazy to hear Anna's name in another man's mouth. Words would lead to shoves, then a bloody massacre involving the Sword of Attila and rancid yak butter.

The doorbell stops. Her bathwater is tepid. Attila disappears with the bubbles. She will dine alone tonight, Indian takeout, lick her fingers of butter chicken, a sexy bachelorette on a little Saturday night.

Only when the last pink curry sauce is cleaned with a swipe of nan does she think to check her phone. She had silenced it, wished it muzzled forever. Locked away in her turret, she doesn't want to hear any more about Christophe stealing the hearts of her class, or her mother's twisted recipes for toe soup, or the neighbour's promises of renewal.

When she listens to the message it's no surprise, more Dotty and her inexplicable family policies. "Pearl needs new underwear, and you can get yourself some at the same time. Maybe replace that ratty housecoat of yours."

And a text. Dotty doesn't text.

"I was at your door. You were busy."

Anna grumbles about her neighbour and his open-door policy until she sees it isn't from him.

"Oh shit."

She looks at the clock. It's too late to call Christophe. Is it too late to call him?

She calls him. Her forehead is wet. Must be the curry spices. Her heart, too much food, acid reflux. No one answers.

"It is late," he says finally.

His voice is deeper at night. I've waited so long, Anna wants to say. "Sorry," she says. Her voice sounds like a child. She says it again, like a professor. "You saw my door."

"Ah," he says. "That door."

"I had it repaired. It works now."

"It is full of locks."

"You wouldn't believe the kooks in the neighbourhood."

"The kooks."

"I was occupied," she says. Her stomach makes her grimace. "Was it important?"

"Things can wait. I am glad to hear you are okay."

"I didn't say I was okay."

"I heard of the…toes." He makes it sound sexy.

"What happened to you?"

"At the skiing? Dmitri said you had gone home. That you abandoned the ski trip, it was too much for you. He called, but you didn't answer. The guide, the Thorbert, he was competitive."

"I'm sorry," Anna says, and hates that she says it. She should know better than to wait for an apology from the French. Algeria still waited.

"I took your class."

Anna bends over on her couch. She should probably hang up. "Uh-huh." Something like a burp escapes her mouth. This is not the cute meet she imagined.

"The students asked about you."

"Sorry," she says. "But Dmitri, I talked to him from the hospital."

"Oh about Dmitri. He offered his sympathies. About your research grant getting turned down."

Well at least somebody finally apologized, or something like it.

"My what? My Spain?"

She watches her tenure track fade before her eyes, like the trails of a skier in a snowstorm.

11. The Limit for Wounded Alpha Males

The sky threw everything it had at the city, and still people refused to believe the gods of winter were malevolent and fickle. Rain, sleet, freezing rain, pellets, hail, snow. Perhaps there were a thousand words for what fell from the sky. Anna left her stone tower in the early morning, her toes wrapped and her boots shuffling across the ice.

But inside Chez Eaton and the underwear department things were just as slippery and depressing. On one side she picked through horribly functional underwear for her aunt, on the other, the being and nothingness of seductive lingerie she'd probably never need. One side already past; the other her inevitable future. She soon left with nothing but an unflattering and comfortable housecoat.

Failing at love she'd got used to. But she'd never failed in her studies. Grants and exams and papers fell as blessings, as tender first snowflakes of fall, as the misty rain of summer nights. She opened her laptop and stared at another paper, *Slut-Shaming in Post-Intentional Phenomenology*. If she wanted to preserve any kind of professionalism, *The Journal of Medieval Whosits* should see this next week. That looked doubtful. She wiped the screen of fingerprints. Behind the file she'd buried other work files, the rejected grant application, next week's class notes. She kept wiping the screen, rubbing it like Aladdin's lamp. Three wishes would be sweet: a finished article, tenure without trial, Christophe come to take her away from all this. She rubbed harder. No knock at the door. Papers and tenure unchanged. No lightning-bolt moment. No one picking out underwear for her, no assisted living.

With one fluid click, she made all her work disappear. What was left on the shiny screen was a title: *The Falcon of the Moor*. Underneath, its unflappable nun Angeles. The nun currently dabbed at the gruesome wounds of the Berber Moor with Egyptian cotton, and only now discovered him to be one-armed, which Anna considered the limit for wounded alpha males.

> He cried out when I gingerly cleansed his chest wound, cursing the one that did this in the tongue we nuns but dimly understood. He sat up and swept my balms and lotions off the table with his one hand, then took hold of my shoulder to push me out the door. But he never pushed. The one-armed Moor could not let go. For all of his privileged life he had kept the common mortal at bay; none ventured near him without elaborate ritual or drawn sword. Now this Christian — this infidel woman! — deigned to reach inside his body, to venture with crude Gothic methods to pull at the vile sickness that tore at his chest.

Anna rocked from side to side, guided by a distant beat from Al-Andalus. When she wrote academic work she rocked back and forth, as if she could urge herself forward. But who wouldn't sway for a one-armed falconer? He had a sizable stump. The falcon loved to perch there. She scrolled down. The Moor made a speedy recovery, all the better to abduct the nun and make a run for it across his known world, Medieval Spain and the Almoravid dynasty. They were in that vague no man's land between Toledo and the Kingdom of Castile.

But that was history. What was needed here was love, caravans of it. With cold blood Anna cut three well-researched paragraphs. Like that she could see the Moor and Sister, free to shuffle up their own dust devils. But could Angeles imagine love with a mere mortal?

> Ten thousand feet high in the air, the falcon carved lazy circles in the hot air. Beneath him, a stubbled land spread in all directions, and distant hovels of men and women appeared irregularly. To the bird, the Moor and horse were but a flutter of circumstance. It descended with patience and devotion. Then at a half-mile's distance from his master's arm, the bird's telescopic vision caught the flash of something in the Spanish sun. In a second the bird stooped to the chase and shot downward at one hundred and fifty miles an hour, the Moor growing ever larger, a rumple of cloth and limbs behind him, until the falcon finally saw that the gleam came from a piece of plain metal lying in the sand, twisted into the shape of a ring.

Oh, that nun! So *transgressive*. Whenever Anna wrote her, her own heart opened and she breathed easier. She looked at the winter weather outside and now thought it playful. Who cared if accuracy suffered? In any Medieval reality, the nun would be a dead woman by now. This was freedom.

> I'd flung the ring I wore as the bride of Christ behind us as we rode. My heart was as twisted as the metal. I told myself that I'd left the ring behind so that others could track us. But what others? The nuns wouldn't leave the abbey to chase down an armed Moor across the semi-arid basin of the Duero. No

one could save me now, and it was my own fault, the fault of my virgin heart.

A tambourine shook, the falcon cried. The bird veered, slowed, and grasped the Moor's stump. The Moor slipped a hood on when the falcon reached for a strip of meat. They had reached the hilltop, and the horse stopped abruptly as the Moor sat up. In the valley below, vultures circled and crested, dining on an army of lost Christians.

I clung to the Moor as he turned the horse around. Now I knew what jangled each time the horse took a step, the tambourine, the call for his raptor, shimmered with every shift of the horse's hip. I imagined he would take me to Cordoba, once we crossed these arid and empty plains. And once there, we would not be able to hold back any longer and our forbidden love would akdhg[ianbv'o

Anna later swore she felt it in her unpainted toenails before she heard the echoes through her house, the way people said they felt lightning come up through the ground while devices crackled snicker and pop. She shivered until her fingers jiggled on top of the keyboard, leaving a trail of confusion. She gaped at the ceiling, prepared for its collapse. Then it hit. An icy roar tore at the roof. Anna squeezed her eyes shut, then peeked through them to what she was sure would be an impossible winter thunderstorm.

Her ceiling was intact. Everything was whole. She'd just convinced herself it was a psychotic incident when the monster bellowed again. Outside her window, a constant veil of white. Anna grabbed the sides of the computer screen she had cleaned so well, spun it away from the window. Her face reflected in it—no makeup. Someone on her roof. And she in a comfortable but unflattering housecoat.

The sound stopped.

"Go away," Anna whispered. A man *in* the house was preferable. Even Attila.

And then she knew. Attila hadn't butchered anyone at her front door. He spared the Zap Reno guy. And now on a weekend morning, that buzzard crawled around on his roof. On *her* roof. A long scrape sent another veil past her window.

Anna pried it open. But kept her head.

"Good morning." She stepped back from the window.

Another scrape. A yell. A crunch.

A slight column of snow fell.

"Are you finished?" Anna winced at each sound.

"I'll be down soon. Need a ladder."

"Because I'm at work here." That sounded authoritative. She would use that tone in the future. With her students.

"It's nothing," Zap said. "I cleared my roof so I thought I'd do yours. You may be short a few slate tiles. I warned you about that. I could help you out there."

"It's too dangerous to shovel up there." That didn't sound authoritative. She sounded like Dotty.

"You kids get down right now," she whispered.

"From this perspective, you know, in the winter. All roofs look alike. Our houses. Though mine isn't slate. Asphalt. Someone was in a hurry I guess. On the subject, I wonder if you could track down that ladder. Some students kicked mine over."

No answer from Anna's window. She froze. Something flew towards Sanjay's window across the street. The snowball missed. Another hit his second-storey dormer. Nobody answered.

"What little person survives up in that attic above Sanjay," Zap said.

Anna had wondered the same thing. "Rochester's mad wife."

"Which Rochester?"

"A piteous creature of Brontë."

"Weren't there three of them?"

"Wives?"

"Broncos."

"Those. Bucked all over the place. All mad, too."

"None of those in your attic, right?"

Sanjay stood below the window now. "You lost your ladder, Mr. Zap. I saw the kids kick it. They do not understand respect."

After much rattling, a ladder finally waved near Anna's window. She grabbed for a throw, but didn't cover the window. She wrapped it around the shoulders of her housecoat, which made her neither invisible nor fashionable. The blood-coloured blanket featured velvet toreadors, a travel gift from Baby Boy Quince. Anna tossed her head to one side, looked away from the rescue ladder like a forgotten paramour.

"She's a writer," Zap explained to Sanjay as he bumped down the rungs. "Romances."

Anna pulled the blanket over her head and waited for the morning to end.

Then she wrote in her head:

> And once there, unable to hold back any longer, our forbidden love would surge up, sweep around me and beneath him and my eyes would fill with relief. Everything would begin. No more wait. No more.

The toreadors went on the window. The shouts and backslapping below faded away. She typed the correction, and switched to the urgent, present tense.

It takes days to unwrap my habit. Each piece of clothing drops from my slight hand and lands behind the Moor's horse on the dune floor with a puff of sand. It is a trail for my pursuers. Or perhaps not. Perhaps he doesn't notice; the few men I had contact with noticed little outside their tiny worlds. He still hasn't touched me. He is too busy keeping an eye out for Christians.

This is not the first time this Moor has transgressed.

We ride towards the first light. That is his goal always. The form that light takes. He tries to explain it to me, but I hear nothing, I drift in and out of sleep behind him. Lost in the folds of his robes. In that world of half dreams, I remember only vaguely the abbey. The demands of the mother superior. The husband I left, the jealous Christ.

It is too light now. The sun pierces the orange groves. He rides deep into them, unfolds me from my perch. My hair falls loose now, and as it brushes against him it transfers shocks through his body. Defenseless like this, unable any more to protest or fight, I reveal the secrets of my beauty. My dark hair coils and rushes like a spring river. The slope of my nose like the Atlas Mountains. The rise of my breasts like small ripe fruits. Among his people the Moor would invent dances for me, sing my praises through the night on the divan of love.

My face rises to his and I cover his mouth with mine. His lips burn like the sand, but I am the lone well in the oasis. The Moor's horse snorts a protest over something, but I cannot stop. The morning sun finds a path through the orange trees and bathes my face and the curls of the Moor. In the heat we tear at our clothes. His scarves. A dagger. My hands clutch at his wide sash. And just when it loosens he catches my hand, and holds it still. We both stop. The cry of a hawk. And I cannot believe it but the Moor pushes me away.

"I cannot further go."

"What?" Anna said. "You're not further going? Can't commit? Or is it the wounds, it's the wounds isn't it. More noble. Like Hemingway. I got news for you, buddy. You're furthering. I might not have a grant, but I will get my man."

The Moor clasped me with his one arm.

"I cannot love you. I cannot bear to see you ever go."

The last woman he couldn't let go of chopped off his arm.

"Shut up," I said. Then I pulled him to me and my lips crushed his, and he dropped his sash and dagger to the sand. Now he wrapped his ~~arms~~ arm around me, now his lips gaped and his tongue drove inside me, driving me on like an animal. Like an animal too my body acted before my mind, and caught on fire. The whole desert was on fire. The smell of burnt almonds and sugar and rosewater.

He seared my bare skin beneath my robes with his touch, and my fingernails dug into his back as he teased the soft folds at my centre. I was a Phoenix consumed in that flame, and at the same time the touch of the ~~Falcon~~ Moor made me born again. My fingers coursed through his raven hair, and I pulled his head back to look deep into his eyes. Then we were lost again in each other's mouths, and my hand involuntarily grasped for the thickness between his legs, to feel exactly how he wanted me. He cried out.

At the same time, the hawk's cry again shattered the sky. It circled over us, caused the hooded falcon to screech in return. "Christians!" the Moor whispered.

In the seconds that followed a hail of arrows scatters through the orange grove. The Moor engulfed me, his hand over my mouth. His skin smells of leather and pine. One of his legs is between mine, pressing me down. I don't resist. I can't. I take fitful breaths through my nose. The ground is warm sand and burst oranges. He looses the pressure on my mouth, and I breathe in a large gulp of hot air. His hand moves. Away from my mouth. Down my neck. Until his fingers curve around my breast and suddenly I am atop the snorting horse, and we gallop deep into sand and sky. The arrows falter, then stop. I glanced behind us. The Moor had stumbled upon my cloister, and I had cared for his wounds, and from that humble accident grew the most extraordinary spiritual confluence of history. I, in love with light; his rhetoric of polished ambiguities. We whispered what no person had yet dared. We searched for words to tell our feelings, and when none came we realized that ours was the first romance. I turned forward to where we rode, and missed the vision of a shimmering genie, a mirage on the dunes, a desert coyote laughing at our messy fates.

12. Are We History?

Christophe stands at the back of the class, Introduction to Love: At First Sight, and frowns at Professor Anna Hill's extrapolations. He thinks her ideas about romance origins simplistic, her theories antagonistic to the logical French view, and her cardigan without form. Her carefully constructed castle of romance could be demolished with a few deft catapults. He wouldn't stay this long in the class if it hadn't been for Dmitri.

The Great Mediator, Dmitri, the Chair. He is responsible again. He did the same thing trying to bring the History Department together in a snow orgy of camaraderie and socialistic democracy, and look where it got them the first time. The woman wandered off and froze her toes. Still walks funny in front of the class. Makes a fool of herself. Dmitri tries again to reconcile his faculty by pushing Christophe to join the class, to encourage scholastic collaboration, but the fool has no idea what the phrase means. At least he hasn't asked him to interact more with students.

This frozen woman, Dmitri told him, the same one who'd snuck into the Paris conference, could use a guiding hand from a more experienced colleague. Up till recently she was on the right tracks towards a professorship, but then a few articles were sent back from journals, and research grants turned down, and now delicate thing has apparently gone off compass again.

Christophe said he would take care of it personally. He specialized in lost women. He didn't say that he left Paris because of such a case, or that the situation had got out of his control, and the lost woman had threatened to point out inconsistencies in his résumé. There was no use detailing every madwoman's trajectory. And Dmitri was so visibly grateful for someone to take the lead. Being a Chair was not all medals and ribbons.

Madame Professor looks grateful too, a senior professor watching over her. This kind of thing is so much simpler than teaching. He could do Dmitri's job much better and with less effort, could use the power to improve this department overnight. Probably a better idea to skip that step completely and become the Dean of Arts. He will see about a Chancellorship later. The thing about going into leadership is that not only does the faculty believe you are a mystery, but that is also your greatest strength. And so Christophe remains at the back of the class, an enigmatic frown on his lips, nods when Anna mentions troubadours, shakes his head at Persian poets.

In her cramped office they watch snow snaking from roofs.

"The problem with this *Journal of Medieval Fluffery* editorial board," she says to Christophe, a rejection letter held up to the cold window, "is that they are unacquainted with the definition of the word creativity." She'd finally finished her *Embodied Erotics* paper, and almost immediately the journal threw it back in her face. "And those that are equate it with the Black Death."

"I heard you singing in your tower."

"In the shower?"

"The tower."

Anna reaches to her desk and closes her laptop with a clean snap. "I don't sing."

"It sounded romantic." He touched her hair, moved it back from her mouth. She licked her lips as if they tickled.

"I'll tell you the truth," she said quickly. "I talk to myself. When I'm writing. My romance novel."

Christophe looked at her and chose not to react. He pretended he heard revelations like that every day. But he would never forget.

"Hobbies are important. But let me help you with your career. The tenure."

She looks out the window. "Wait. One thing at a time. You're loitering under my turret?"

"I was not under your turret. I was first on the balcony." He steps towards her. As he expects, she doesn't move away.

"It's not the first journal to reject me. I've got a history." This is a lie.

"You are a woman of mysterious levels."

"That doesn't mean anything."

"But your premise is misguided. Romance was born with the love between vassal and lord, not with Arab transformers."

Outside the late afternoon sun descends, and students wander off the campus with their collars turned up against the wind. She turns on her desk lamp. In the window's reflection Professor Hill's harsher edges are softened.

"It would only take some tweak."

He's close enough to breathe on her ear. "Some tweets?"

"For your tenure."

This is what careers came down to in this university. Tweaks and tweets. Refusals and rejections. Last week, Christophe had to laugh when Schoplik from Economics was denied tenure because his work outside the university was too popular. Not enough time on university research.

"If you need to go to Spain, *vamos a España*." He touches her shoulder. Lost women love to be spontaneous. When they're ready. "I know a ski refuge in los Picos de Europa."

Anna grimaces. He moves his hand to her twists of hair, and she pulls away.

"If I'm going to Spain I don't want to see snow."

His fingers brush her neck, underneath her hair.

"Tomorrow. We will go now. We will ski. Alone, away from the noisy Alps. Can you see it?"

But he knows, of course she can see it. She's seen it for months. Naked on furs in front of the fire. But she pulls away again. Does she still blame him for her getting lost in her own land?

"Professor Hill," says Christophe. His lips by her ear.

That's all he needs to say. Anna presses against the window, her arms crossed in front of her. Christophe lets his hand drop from her shoulder. They stand in full view of the commons and the students battling snow. Anna jerks back from the window, into Christophe. Surely she can feel him through his well-cut trousers. All of him. He tugs on the cord of her desk lamp.

"Anna."

He insists.

This is not how she imagined it. The lighting is wrong. Her office smells of unfinished work, rushed lunches, afternoon headaches. Voices echo in the hallway. The door is unlocked. But isn't it too appropriate, professors uncovering love in a centre of learning? Anna's shoulders tense. She could see Audrey waving a Complaint Template, Form A-09, talking about assessors, Disciplinary Action, impaired educational performance. And who was the harasser—the one with the grey cardigan. Anyway, nothing has happened. Only hot breath, some incidental brushing against the breast. A name, softly chanted in a deep accent. All her clothing still on. Children, groping in a schoolyard. Anna sees herself twenty-five years ago or more. She stands in a damp alley between buildings, lifts her skirt and knows she should feel shame, but doesn't, she feels wide open, plunged into the world of adults and the endless possibility that Grown Up offers…and the boy runs away.

Christophe is no boy. No fumble and grasp. A European man spared the rod god of Puritans, a century or two of rebellion behind him. Experienced, experimented, and a few *exes* besides. His hand barely outlines the curve of her breast as he mumbles *des mots d'amour, des mots de tous les jours*. A finger falls to her lips and she takes it in her mouth. Accidentally, she hopes. Everything is an accident with her eyes closed. His fingers drop to her neck, the brush of an archaeologist uncovering statuary. He pulls her to him and his fingers tighten till the room spins. Her frozen toes are numb. From the sky above comes the cry of a hawk. She is the rhythm of a rosary in his fingers. For the increase of faith; for the increase of hope; for the increase of love. Oh Lord, open my lips… the cry of the hawk again. Anna gasps for breath.

"Anna!"

Her door is half open. A grizzly bear on his hind legs, pawing at the door frame. Great heaves of breath. The muzzle comes round. "Anna," Dmitri exhales. He's run all the way from the head office at the end of the hall, but when he looks up to see Anna limp in Christophe's arms his hunt is forgotten. Does everyone in this chamber hear the echo of his heart? He must find his breath. Dmitri leans against the wall, stares at the floor, makes post hibernation grunts. Christophe stands in front of him.

"Will you die?"

"Not yet." Dmitri looks up at Anna. Finally one side of her mouth smirks. She coughs. The Frenchman's hands.

"In your turret." Dmitri exhales operatically.

"We can do this later," Christophe says.

Anna tries to read Dmitri's eyes. Does he only see more paperwork, Form A-09, or does he worry that what he's seen is not harassment, and that paperwork is the least of his worries?

"What's wrong with my turret?"

"Through window. But. You have no problem, they work on it now."

"Who they?"

"The man who claims to be your husband."

Anna rubs her neck.

"A charmed man," Dmitri says. "Good jokes. Protects your house from trees."

13. First Response

The kiss was an accident.

They'd rushed to the parking garage. Christophe would drive her through the growing snowstorm to her turret. She'd forgotten her purse in the hurry, and so her house keys. Turned back to get them, came to the garage with her hair sprung free and frizzed in the wet snow. And now underground among the melted snow and coughing cars Christophe's crisp navy shirt still smelled of early September. The cement pillars and floors had an odor of mocha. Top notes of ginger.

He leaned to put her bag in the back seat. Anna fell towards him, wanted her purse near. He turned back and their lips brushed. Maybe it was their cheeks. Panic ecstatic, Anna yanked a book out of her bag and flapped its pages in front of Christophe's face. "What was that?"

"What?" He punched buttons on the dash.

She couldn't name it. Anna held the book in front of her.

"You will know when I kiss you." An opera aria floated from the speakers.

"My house."

"I am not a student. Should I kiss you?"

Her hands twitched. A moment later she hit him on the forehead with the book. Only a paperback. She held it tight. The reviews on the back cover grew blurry in her eyes. Underneath it, Christophe's breath blew hot and long. Far away a car's tires protested in a tight turn. His breath was mature wine. When did he find time to drink at school? She lowered the book. His eyes on her. Too focused. She lifted the book again but he threw it and grabbed her hair and pushed her mouth onto his.

The paperback romance lodged under the seat, forgotten for weeks, a talisman.

The diva hit the high notes and everything spun. The garage. The car tires. Christophe reversed and squealed. A horn sounded and they went forward too fast and when he finally let her go they squealed again and she ducked uselessly. Anna groped her seatbelt as they skidded to the pay booth. Out the door and aloft over the sidewalk and into a foot of powder. Landed and spun, bounced off the curb and swung a dancer through the street, a tail of honks and screams behind them. And inside the car: "What the fuck!"

She demanded he slow down, it was a house, a turret, nobody dying—not at the house anyway. And where was he going? The house was just a few blocks that way.

"I will take you to the airport, and then to Spain."

"The airport isn't this way."

"We will go where the snow blows us." On the Autoroute 10 on the edge of the seaway, too fast but finally straight, she loosened her grip on the door handle and her mind. She remembered suggesting they stop, when suddenly the sky darkened and a hail of longbow arrows began bouncing off the car, which headed straight towards the water's edge. In a vague distance she heard screaming: "Take cover! The Christians have found us!"

But they were safe in the car against those medieval arms. Whoever had ordered the assault did not know the Moor and his nun. Religions could not interfere. What grew between them was a declaration of decency between a man and woman. They were under attack from those who could not understand the eternal possibilities of romance.

In that car, headed towards that guard rail, the world would change. The shift would happen in increments. Nobody would notice at first. A kiss. A poem would spread through traffic. A promise everlasting. On the commute home, lives would change. Wives would come home to husbands not with bread and milk but with heaven in their hearts. Children would capture fireflies and teach them to sing. Fathers would return from unholy wars and never leave. And it would all have begun here, in the seconds before the car burst through the confines of the road and dove to the murky unconscious of the seaway.

And they would witness the transformation, the infidels. They would lay down their pikes and swords and crossbows, make of them a pyre and watch them burn till the smoke curled around the penthouses and watchtowers. Up from the seaway, over the Pont Champlain, down the 15 past the suburbs and farms and over the New York border, a tsunami of *caridad* would wash away the emptiness and fill the world anew.

"Stop."

He slammed the brakes. The world sped up again and spun in snow whirlwinds. Cars out the window spilled in all directions until with a gentle nudge she and Christophe bumped up against a barrier. Fading horns in the distance. An opera chorus.

"What do you want?"

Anna couldn't speak yet. She tried even breaths, slowed her heart. She remembered her turret lay in ruins.

"What does everybody want?" Louder this time, through a Bellini flourish. Backed by a steady rhythm of cars. One hand loose on the wheel. The other tapped buttons as the opera got louder. His eyes stared ahead, then closed as the diva plucked the remaining notes from her sheets. His free hand bobbed to conduct. Anna turned to him. Those were tears.

Paris. That was what she wanted. Not Spanish mountains, or grants, or tenure. She missed their Paris and didn't know anyone in Paris and she didn't have any money to move to Paris, but it was all. She needed to tell him. That Spain and history and gender had all been an accident, that she'd never found the logic to settle on the Seine. That a life of adventure and love—or peace and contentment, she wasn't sure—but to be kissed, and to risk her life as she knew it…

"I want to go home," she said.

They didn't go home. They didn't go to Spain. He kissed her.

Chainsaw rumbles at his feet, a whiff of gasoline in the air, on the floor an accident of blood-red oil: she will find him like this. While he wraps his arms around the trunk of a three-ton intruder, a lovesick lumberjack. Seventy-five-inch circumference, easy.

Soon, he figures, she'll walk in and catch her ginger soufflé hair in the branches. Jackson Zaporzan cleans his fingernails with twigs and rubs sap over blistered hands. A hero in blue coveralls. Things in hand. Another heritage building rescued.

Snow still snakes through the roof. Frost crackles down branches, nestles on twigs that sprout loose-leaf papers from Anna's desk. On the floor a paper mosaic shifts. Zap's finger dusts frames on the wall, watches the women in photos shimmy. All those maidens and no texture of man in the room. He shuts down the chainsaw and slides through Anna's new forest, fingers locked behind his back. The shattered frames he brushes into a pile. Showers them into a box. They are aunts with secrets, grandmothers never met. Loves realized and love with mold on the edges. He plucks tiny shards from the ends of his fingers when finished with the broken frames and with a sleeve, wipes the wall of his blood path.

Slow. Sharp. Separation. He'd heard it from his shop behind the house. The unnatural break-and-enter through the turret window. In jeans and undershirt he'd ignored the cold, and with one step into the courtyard identified the beast. Icicles flaked off its branches and teased the hair on his arms. He would not shiver. Slate tiles lay in the snow beside shattered wood. Zap couldn't see the base of the tree from there, but it didn't matter. He didn't consider how it fell. He considered how to fix it. The tree had missed his roof, but a snapped branch lay in front of his shed. At first he thought it was an abandoned antler. Felt the contours with his bare hands, flexed it to test the humidity, scanned it for disease. He stowed it inside the workshop among the warm odor of cold storage. Zap gassed up the chainsaw, collected a space heater and extension cord, and pulled on his coveralls. Left a message with the history department. She would be there in minutes. He didn't know what he could accomplish by then, but the important thing was a first response. Medical. Ecological. Emotional.

Forty-five minutes on she still hasn't showed. He wouldn't leave his house wounded and alone for so long. If he cleans up too well she'll never know how he's saved it. But over the days, the weeks (these tree invasions took time), she would see his innate craftsmanship. And he would see her. They would see each other. They would see through each other. She would let him see inside her, and he would let her see inside him, and when he held her... when they took off their clothes.... Something knocks on the house. But it isn't her door. The tree settling on the roof. Or his helper in the next room.

"What you doing? Get in here." An orange cat pads into the turret. Rochester, né Buster. Cat follows him everywhere anyway, no matter what name he uses. They argue, but the cat never loses. Zap bends to start the chainsaw again and Rochester flees. Better if they're too busy to notice Anna arrive. More natural like.

Because she is natural, he knows that, and it all comes out in her bushfire hair. Zap pulls branches away, leaves them in a corner. That is attractive, that simplicity underneath the professorial coating. If he'd studied psychology, maybe he could tell himself why. But he hasn't studied psychology, hasn't studied much of anything in school. So he doesn't tell himself a thing, only cuts branches, and when a pile gets too unwieldy he binds it together with thinner branches. The cat crawls into one, so Zap fashions an exit near the top. One of the few things he does remember about school is his English Lit teacher in junior high, when he was alone with her in the classroom and stood in the sunlight beside her wood desk and breathed in the musky perfume that rose from the desktop or the pencil shavings or the perfume between her breasts, because he hadn't read an assigned book and never read any books, and she was curt with him, and for a reason he couldn't remember his young boyself began to cry. That comes back to him now, while he kicks fallen twigs together and cuts back this beast. What department is that memory from—History, Psychology, Education?

Still no sound at the door. Branch piles fill the turret so he piles them in corners of other rooms, around windows, down stair railings. He threads through with ladders and ropes and a plastic tarp that sends Rochester scrambling to a corner. The cat is skeptical. Unblinking eyes look at the hole in the ceiling, then at Zap. Fur fluffs with a shake. You can see your breath in this room. Pick out distant sirens in the city, hear the old wind wheeze.

Maybe he looks like a monster, from a cat's-eye view. Up on a ladder, draped in plastic, a ten-foot blue cryptid with flapping wings. Grunts and groans and mutters as he struggles to close the hole. But Rochester smells Zap, that old wood and leather smell, with a stain of dark chocolate and a memory of grilled steak, and so he stays. Tiny drifts form in the edges of the turret before Zap fills the hole and sheds his monster.

Zap stands back with cold hands in pockets and nods. Rochester disagrees. The patch is garish and noisy and the winter wants in.

"It's temporary," Zap explains.

You the king of temporary, Rochester says.

"It's necessary. Where is she?"

Rochester cleans snow dust off his paw. He believes Zap has not done a solid job on purpose.

"You can't burst into someone's house and make permanent changes."

Because then they won't need you back.

"This from a professional at making people need them."

Nobody forced you to feed me. Rochester tucks his legs under his body.

"Speaking of sustenance, I wonder if our Anna has a little something in the fridge."

Coffee-flavoured yogurt and yellowing arugula and grape jam. Zap spreads some of the jam on rice cakes and breaks off bits for

Rochester, who is unconvinced and holds out for thin-sliced raw fondue beef. You know the kind, Rochester says, that falls apart in your mouth? None of that there?

"Or carpaccio," Zap says, lifting the cat onto the counter. "Or any flesh at all. How does she make it through the winter?"

Without conviction Zap searches for a beer, even a warm one. Two hours have passed since he left a message at the university. He makes do with an open bottle of white wine, foregoes a glass to avoid doing dishes. He doesn't want to be presumptuous.

Back upstairs the tarp still flaps, but with the door closed, that world is contained. The bulk of the tree trunk still rests against the outside of the house. Tomorrow. Proper equipment. And the owner present. A few papers still flutter in the branch piles. Zap begins to pluck them from the enchanted forest. He only glances at the words before stuffing them into Rochester's former hiding hole. A fine nest.

A book hides under the remains of Anna's jumbled desk. Something about Construction on the cover. He bends down to retrieve it. Rochester joins the investigation. Stuck in as a bookmark, a ripped piece of lined paper. Zap pulls it out. A name (Auntie Pearl), a phone number (Montreal). Sticks it in his pocket.

That was a marker, Rochester says. Is there for a purpose.

"Knowing where you are is overrated."

They argue about this regularly. Discord began with Rochester's insistence on leaving his mark. Zap is more in favour of the brain's ability to abstract territory. Rochester counters that this is all well and good if you have a prefrontal cortex. Zap wonders why if cats have such an acute sense of smell they have to leave such exaggerated markers.

What's the book, Rochester says. Don't debate something you're ignorant of.

Zap scanned the back of the book. "Sounds like fun. 'When otherwise pure Christian crusaders grilled and devoured dead Muslims'...what the... 'the true birth of Arthurian romance lies in cannibalism. After reading this brilliant book, you will never read Medieval banquet scenes the same again.'

Zap looked at the title. *Empire of Flesh*. He threw the book as if it had bitten him, and Rochester had to scurry again.

"Sounds like your kind of romance," Zap said. "In the alley, middle of the night."

I'm sorry we didn't find that carpaccio now.

Zap tugs at a loose end of the plastic tarp, and Rochester finds a branch hideaway. Anyway, the cat suggests, we all follow instincts. Though some instincts are more productive than others.

"Sounds like someone might need to be fixed."

Rochester is ready to rebut that it ain't broke, but he has lost Zap's attention. After the disappointment of the cannibal romance book, Zap is focused on a new find. He looks over his shoulder. Door open. Silent downstairs, still. Her loss if she doesn't come home right away when her house is under attack. He'll clean up a few things. Like this, hanging on the wall beside the broken shelf. Something mannish, finally. A leather bag curls at the corner flaps, clasps of brass, much too heavy to hang off a nail that size. He lifts it. The nail comes along, and a puff of panel board dust too. Zap traces his steps back to Anna's solid wood chair and peels back the flap.

More paper. These people. He lifts out the first leaf, printed with a title. In the dark of winter's early sunset it's difficult to read. He holds it under the desktop lamp that struggles on the same extension cord as the space heater. *The Moor of the Falcon*. The title is crossed out and underneath is handwritten *The FalconMoor*. Beneath that, printed in a luxurious font: by Anna Eden Hill.

"Eden," he says out loud. A spell descends on the turret, snow turns to bougainvillea petals, walls give way to palms and vines and Mount Royal outside evolves into a South Pacific waterfall wrapped in bands of mist and sun. Zap pulls out the rest of the pages. Birds pass by the window, begin as pigeons and end as parrots. Each page is pulled and flipped; fingers are licked, DNA left.

It takes forty-five minutes and the rest of the bottle of white wine, whose bouquet is greatly helped by the persistent smell of cut tree. The snow in the corners of the turret turns to rivulets and he has no thought of being caught or surprising Anna. Rochester is asleep in a branch tower. But Zap figures it out. Out of all he reads and skims and rereads, he returns always to the same clear meadow:

> his hand over my mouth smells of leather and pine. His leg is between me, pressing down. I don't resist.

This trap of pages from the pulp of Anna's heart: it is him.

14. Anna Eden Elsewhere

Christophe holds her shirt in his hands. He hovers over the sink. His kitchen. Anna Eden elsewhere, *in media res*.

Perhaps she could have spent more on lingerie. On his sofa she'd resisted him with feral instinct, and made him baptize his mohair blanket and her in serious Pomerol, a full glass on her white silk.

He brings the shirt to his face. Forest fruits, vanilla, racy.

She says she can't smell it fully. But she stands there in brassiere, shivering as the ice clicks outside on the window. Bordeaux. He had pulled her rusty red ringlets and he knew she liked it. Christophe held the silk in one hand, saddened by waste, captivated by aromas of minerals and clays, the welcoming nose of a nervous woman with mocha undertones and a mouthful of plump fruits on the palate. Ready to drink now, may be cellared for later.

Her breasts moist from wine or fear. Her body looks ready for emergency, at the least. He licks her shoulder. Her temperature rises three degrees.

Her phone has buzzed the whole time she's been here. Dmitri again, or her mother. She hopes they will all go away.

"I'm starving," she says.

He produces a bottle of two-year-old Muscadet, neutral as Switzerland. Christophe empties the white over the stain, the only method he uses. Never too expensive. Not Champagne. *Wine comes in at the mouth.* When his hands touch her he watches. He watches her skin flinch, blood rise to colour flesh. *Love comes in at the eye.* And when his fingers glide through her hair again he senses her short sharp breath come back. Hiccups. *That's all we shall know for truth.* He pushes her hips against the sink on that drenched silk. *Before we grow old and die.*

Anna's mind flips. Her head pulled to him. Her scalp burns. The title of her book shimmers in a marquee above the sink: THE FALCONMOOR. The cold blues of reality turn to the yellows of sepia. Christophe without all the costume of that first party, naked of beard or turban. How can she even think of her book when… still those kisses at the shoulder. The book falls away for an instant. She grabs at it—the Moor would kiss the nun's shoulder, and… dance, music, merrymaking… instruments on the divan of love.

What he wants. What every man wants. Moor or Christian. Well she wouldn't give him that, not like that. Not after all that waiting of hers, those washouts in Paris and Montreal and the stark plains of the Kingdom of León… all she wants is more of that on her collarbones. She shakes her head. Her hair tumbles into lips, and she grabs back at the Moor's hair. No, Christophe's hair. The transgression. The love of light. His words now, French and low, a prayer of longing.

She wants to laugh now. Not politely, she wants to impregnate him with laughter. Even as his hand traces a half moon. She has drunk the potion of Pomerol, and its heat and tickle have found her nerves. Her phone buzzes again, imitating her synapses.

"You have to know something," she says.

"*Le temps des discours est terminé.*"

It's true. She shouldn't lecture. Something about his need to limit her frees her. She will let go and live this moment, imagined and sculpted for years. His pale skin, fingerprints on her lips. Rougher than she remembers. The dry of winter, and too many pages turned, and a man's aversion to hand cream. Are her hands rough like that too, cracking in the cold? And the wooden arm of this sofa is cold as well of course, he is French, he doesn't understand central heating. And her without a top on stainless steel sink and drenched in crushed grapes. His chin scratches too. She feels every whisker in her pores. On his tongue the lees of that same Pomerol brings her back to Dotty's basement and the first stolen sips with a pimply boyfriend. Anna shivers too long, and Christophe scratches his nails down her spine until she growls at him. She should say something. They should get under covers. She should leave.

> We trembled in each other's arms. The shocking desert night, its inability to retain heat. He had kidnapped me, stolen me from my hiding place in the orange groves. But when he saw the roundness of my breasts his face turned a burgundy colour that climbed from his breastbone to his chin. I was the corrupter in that deserted castle that night. I unveiled the eyes of the FalconMoor.

A deserted castle. Her turret. The tree.

"I have to go."

And when his hands only hold her tighter as her clothes fall, she doesn't resist, she wants to dive into that orange grove. Or at least wake to offered orange juice in the morning. Even as he grasps her throat and her head snaps back into his chest, as she hears that cheap lingerie tear. Even when her breaths shorten, even when she struggles to stand upright and he pushes her down, even when on the side of her head she feels his hand hit her in an unforgiving slap.

Danger in the desert. They were never alone. As he found her heart, an assassin leapt from behind an olive tree and grabbed her. A Christian, a heretic, come to think he'd save her, and the nun screaming as she's torn from her love....

"Wait, wait." Her voice hoarse. This is not imagination. But his hands leave her throat. The room pulses as she fills her lungs. She is over his knee. Her lingerie is ruined. He wears all his clothes but he is naked and she reaches for him, and her clothes on the floor buzz. Her telephone has no mercy or shame. She would let the bells chime, resound with alarm.

"Answer your *putain de téléphone*. Or I will." He reaches to the floor.

"Leave it." She is in no position to argue, but it is her training.

"Everyone wants you. Dmitri. That neighbour. Your mother." He kicks at her clothes and the phone slides across the room. "Stop." Anna gathers herself among the mohair blanket. All those people in the room with them now. She scoops up the clothes and the phone and locks the bathroom door behind her, props her back against it. She holds the phone so tight in one hand it cramps, and the other hand's fingers curl into her palms. When she loosens her grip the rest of her body relaxes too, and a wave of warmth descends from her belly again. She squeezes her legs together. Her skin still shivers without a touch. How could she let… it's the new millennium goddammit, a woman doesn't… she had to pee. Her panties are ripped. She pulls them off and buries them under tissue in the garbage can. How much did they cost? Do they refund for things like this? The phone buzzes beside the sink. What if it's the police. One bra strap is gone too. What if it's an emergency? Of course it's an emergency. A tree is in her turret. She digs the panties out of the garbage and stuffs them in a pocket. Or someone is hurt. Bleeding. Naked.

She puts herself together and shivers when the cold stained silk shirt sticks to her shoulder. No sound comes from outside the door. She will freeze but will go to her university office and regroup. And what will he do if she says something, to someone. What will he strangle? What can he deny, what can he ruin, what tenure track can he derail?

"Are you all right?"

The inquiry of a harmless scholar.

"Do you have bad news? You suddenly ran away when you checked your phone."

"You hurt me."

"You hurt yourself. The phone message. I am worried about you."

Had she checked the message first? Hadn't she run from it? Or from Christophe.

"I can't read my phone. My head is spinning."

"You head is spinning because of the message. Let me in."

Anna says nothing. Did she read the message? She knew a little about trauma. Events got mixed up. Yet she is sure her phone is still in her purse. She is sure Christophe assaulted her.

"I never did," he says. "You would know."

She digs out her phone. The text says: Your family has disappeared.

15. Elopement Protocol
(or, A Thousand Suns)

This was the lesson Jackson Zaporzan learned from his family, his father renovator of swank Westmount homes, who learned it from his father before him in the Old Country where he built pre-fab Khrushyovkas, who learned it from his father before him who built dachas on the shores of the Black Sea, and so on back to the Cossacks and the Golden Horde and Scythians who all built and renovated their histories, this was the lesson: Beware free borscht. He could not spend all day on volunteer work in Anna's turret. His mobile had the day fully booked, and reminded him with chirps and gurgles of imminent doom.

    His scheduled tour of historic architecture in the Coleridge Park ghetto had already been canceled. Attendance was notoriously sparse for the city's cruelest months. Didn't bother him, though. Got his best ideas in the snow without nuts around.

    Instead, as part of his community service (a chance to "return the compliment" to the neighbourhood after a forgettable misdemeanor) he scheduled an impromptu tour outside the strictures of the Coleridge Park Architectural Preservative Society, to parts beyond the student ghetto. In a blizzard. Wasn't what he called a blizzard though. This was snowfall. You'd know it when you were in a Montreal blizzard. You'd know when it smacked you. So there they were, he and a friend who was delighted with his proposal, well protected for the occasion and in the snow-diffracted lights of a truck, looking at architecture. His friend said something and Zap agreed, but truth was he hadn't understood one mumble. Her layers of scarves and furry hoods conspired against it. You could only see a slit for eyes, but they were delighted.

<hr/>

"She's disappeared," Dotty said. "She *is* your family. We have such a small family. Will you find her?"

"Wandering is an expression of a real desire," the Director at La Falaise Manor for Assisted Living said. Anna was on her phone, in a taxi headed there. "We all have fundamental needs that aren't always met."

"I'd say the fundamental need is to keep her out of this blizzard."

"I understand that. We try to keep exit-seeking to a minimum, by keeping things interesting inside the building. Her primary need is companionship. We encourage the family to visit."

Did everyone try to put the blame on her? "Obviously our elopement protocol is to do everything we can. Rooms have been searched. Hospitals called. Police notified."

Where would Pearl wander, lost in her mind, frozen to her toes? She hadn't lived in Montreal for decades. When she found Pearl, Anna would take her out of there. She would be more caring too, and she would listen to her. They would be friends. Christophe would see that Anna had a maternal instinct, that… There was a bustle of noise beyond the Director.

"There she is! All bundled up and warm. *Bonjour Madame Perle!*"

The Director said she looked fine, all smiles and nonsense as usual. Apparently a family member *had* come by to provide companionship. Your husband! He was already gone, such a caring and humble man.

Anna said La Falaise knew best how to take care of her aunt, and after she redirected the taxi home she said she'd try to come by later that evening if she could cancel a few things, work out a schedule with her *husband*.

He was parking his truck in front of his house when she jumped out of the taxi and informed Zap he was lucky she didn't press abduction charges, and that the police were notified all the same, and who did he think he was anyway, kidnapping her aunt. And Zap said it was time she was back home taking care of her house and her loved ones. And wondered why nothing distracted her from whatever was so important at the French professor's house.

Then Anna asked him why he knew so much about her life and aunt and what was he inferring.

So Zap said he inferred about Anna more than almost anything else in the world. And he'd found the name and number in her *Fleshy Empire Cannibal Romance* book. And Rochester told him to pursue his instinct.

Then no one spoke for a long time.

Zap said he and Pearl had talked about Anna, like about how you had to love yourself before anyone else did. You've got altogether too much to say, Anna said. Then she regretted saying that. And Zap said that if she didn't stop putting her foot in her mouth soon she'd swallow everything that was told her. Then Anna started to say something about his anatomical logic and if he kept talking there was a likelihood of her foot in *his* mouth. Then she breathed in, and said that maybe sometimes she did explain too much but it was an occupational hazard, and if he didn't want to learn something he should shut up. And Zap said he already learned enough for one day, especially about her atomic logic bombs.

The phone rang and Anna stopped herself from throwing it into the snowbank.

"I'm calling to see if everything goes well. You left so quickly. I so hope it wasn't bad news."

Who is this, she wanted to say. Who are you?

"Your aroma is still all over me."

Anna shivered, could still feel the red and white wines on her blouse. She smelled like a French village in September.

"Come back. We'll go see your house together. We'll make sure you're safe. I worry about you. Your behavior. Erratic."

Did he mean erotic? *"I worry about me."* It was time she thought about herself.

"I need you."

I don't need to spend much time with my aunt, Anna thought. Maybe regular phone calls. Those end-of-term papers would pile up soon.

Zap, who stood beside her the whole time in his furry ear cap, now touched her head. "That's a fresh red bruise," he said. "You want me to put some ice on that." He started scooping up a snowball.

"Ice is the problem," Anna said. "I slipped."

Anna dismissed Zap without thanks, watched him skip up the stairs to Sanjay's to perform ritual male greetings with their secret handshakes and clown banter. But she craved her own rituals, alone with the magic of black-and-white channels and extravagant socks over tender toes. She groaned when she saw her door encircled by a tangle of branches. Her broken house and Zap's intervention were no longer deniable.

A cat in her window reminded her that avoidance was futile. She did not own a cat. Since a certain Prozac dachshund incident, she'd sworn off pets altogether. In the same way she now swore off all visiting professors, every inferring carpenter, and the gamut of quaint grannies. But the cat didn't move from its nest of curtain and branch. He taunted her, challenged her to enter the breached fortress.

The precarious maple had disappeared with its shadow. The house felt empty, like after a roommate skips out on the rent. The only clue, golden sawdust outside. The worst way to end a day already too full of action and denouement.

The cat leapt from window to frayed Moroccan rug, dagger claws and a sabre tail. He'd probably scaled the trunk assault tower, and found a fissure through the tree hole. And what other treacherous beasts stormed with it? In a great sigh, the cat rolled on its back and began an orange and rotund purr.

"Hello?"

Her umbrella stand overflowed with fresh cut maple branches in water. Behind the cat was a construction of green limbs fashioned into a doll's wood cabin, or maybe a hasty pile of firewood. Tiny enough for a professor (assistant) to manipulate. If a professor had a proper fireplace to burn it in.

Everywhere branches and twigs entwined her doorways and windows, sprung from containers, graced arches. She felt a tail hook her ankle, nudged it away while it rubbed back harder. Anna opened the front door, shooed it out, but instead it bolted upstairs for her turret. She understood. She wanted that too: a shredded sweater and those socks and wait for the winter's siege to deplete its ammunition. Never rise again till thaw. Only she knew upstairs there was a disaster and a feral animal lost among it.

Anna's education evaded biology when possible, but even so she knew to worry about all that defrosted wood in the middle of winter. From a sick tree, felled by a tender blizzard, peopled by battalions of bugs and beetles on the march, and a flea-infested stray who caressed it all. A Plague waiting to happen. She wound up the stairs, danced by the vases and jars of twigs. One lay on its side already, felled by the cat. She tracked the wet footprints.

Raw wood enveloped her on the second floor, along with a fresh draft of February air. Sweet and acrid, it launched her sneezes. The first one flushed the cat from the bathroom. With the second it tore into her turret office. The breeze came from there. She nudged the door with her fingertips and sneezed a last time. In front of the turret window one pane gone, covered with tight plastic. Above it, quick-fixed patches of plywood on the roof. But around the window a string of patio lights twinkled in the dim room, and on either side of the bench under the window, piles of logs rose halfway up the wall. Books knocked out of her crushed shelves lined the room too, multi-coloured watchtowers of history that guarded against future attack. What remained of her desk cowered among the logs and in its place wobbled an unfamiliar wooden table and chair, bare of all paper and technology. The corpse of her computer lay shattered in a box, a note taped to the top: RIP. But still on the wall in its rightful place her father's satchel bulged with romance. She stood in a rustic cabin, a lumberjack's retreat, jury-rigged with aromas and random patches.

The cat hooked her ankle. This time she curled down and wrapped him up in her arms. Anna held him long enough to read the medallion: a phone number, and the words Feed Me.

She glided to the new table and let the cat pour off her forearms, land without fanfare on its front paws and stay there, a gypsy saltimbanco. The table rocked as he lay down. Anna pulled out the chair. The cat offered his belly and they talked that way for a long time, of bellies and fur, of atomic secrets hung on walls, of the need to divulge an ache so deep that she could imagine a carpenter touching her pages, her thousand suns, uncovering her love more than she ever could. Anna never did find her sweater her socks her black-and-white, but instead went to bed with a constant purr on her breast. The payoff from a quick side trip to the kitchen for Feed Me. And almost forgot about the tree that lay in her turret or the lips that fell to her mouth, or the purpling bruise on her temple.

16. Sympathetic and Contagious Magic

The weekend arrived in her treehouse; in a treehouse, it was always the weekend. This was not always desirable, because while the front ends of weekends were glorious and free, the back ends tended towards nostalgia and dread. Halfway through their short lives, they turned and ate their own tails. Anna was at the magic hour now, one minute before midnight on a Saturday and still nestled in the novelty of exploring her transformed house. She found enough stability to sit herself down and face some truths. Unfortunately, by the time she unveiled the first truth, time flipped by midnight and began its descent to the darker side.

The singular truth grew from the colour purple that blossomed on her temple, amplified by her makeup mirror. The bruise kept her dizzy and unable to concentrate on her work. She did not need more distractions than she already had on the road to tenure. The dizziness was not the result of suffering a bump on the head, but on her not being sure what or who caused it.

It was true that the purple appeared after she left Christophe's house, and before she saw Zap. There had been passion at Christophe's, there had been uncontrollable desire. Before she saw Zap there had been ice on the streets, and the panic of trying to find her aunt. All of these truths were immersed in the pressure cooker that was an assistant professor on tenure track, trying to get noticed for the right things, and to do those things perfectly. Then the mix was seasoned with the still painful memory of her disastrous skiing episode, which she saw now was all her fault, and the stale spice of her mother repeating, during her awkward years, You clumsy girl! So that by the time Anna limped to bed and carefully covered her toes with the blanket, she believed that her purple was evidence of an eager but artless woman, and a man whose adoration was ferocious when she stood before him half naked and unveiled. His ardour wasn't always understandable, but it was appreciated.

He wasn't appreciated. He knew that, acknowledged it, and moved on. One didn't spend one's career and life trying to be liked, like some American cheerleader blowing all the boys over. Since he'd left Paris—and he admitted this to himself in the dark of a Saturday night, with no woman at hand—he had to prove to these imbeciles that he was a man, to stand before them and crow like a *coq* in the morning announced to the world what was his and what would be his. The *students* were the issue, those tendrils of hormone and moan, the university would be vastly improved without them. The idea came to him quite naturally as he erased the students from the classroom (keeping only the prettiest for his bedroom fantasies), and spread the university's good will to the world beyond, the adult world. If they would give him charge of the place, if he would Chair, or better of course if he would Dean, well if he would be Chancellor, Mighty God, Everlasting Father, Prince of Peace. Yes, that had the right sound. He lay on his back in bed and spread his legs, his toes protruding from the blanket and his hand of its own accord searched for his centre, his essence, his rule.

The university would reach out and touch the community. Influence would be greater, and history, glorious history would seep into the everyday, and the past would finally be present. He would bring in others, welcome the sociologists, psychiatrists, anthropologists, and just to show how inclusive he could be, the scientists and their cold worlds. He would fashion *la Grande université McGill*, and so what if it was blatant thievery from the French President and *le Grand Paris*. It was a time for action, for the suburbs were afire, and none but he could put them out.

Christophe held his cock, erect and hard in his loving hand. What he was, was a champion, a champion for women, minorities, queers. He was the progressive face of the twenty-first century, and he would need a woman beside him to show the world his taste and power. He saw himself on the dias speaking to the city, and that young teacher's assistant beside him, her long dark hair and pillow lips, her eyes looking up to him as saviour and guide all knowing, and whatever he believes she believes, whatever he touches she shall touch, he would grab that dark hair and pull her head down to him in front of any crowd, she would take him in her mouth and swallow him because he so desired. But in his fantasy, the TA kept flickering and changing into another woman, older, smarter, thinner lipped. He resisted. He summoned the young girl again and she looked up at him but her eyes became Anna's, the professor and her shapeless cardigan, her unkempt hair, her wine-stained skin.

He came into his hand, his mouth full of curses.

By Sunday morning the glow faded. Perhaps it was literal. The sky was grey, the sun hidden, Anna's housecoat beige. Whatever the reason, Anna at breakfast had only one goal for the day, and that was to clean her house. And by that she meant that someone would clean it for her. Cleaning meant not only throwing out the rotting branches and infested wood, but also repairing the damage. She faced and squarely dealt with things last night (though this morning they remained unnamable, securely *things*), and she now saw that the tree was the last thing remaining between her and tenure. Once that was taken care of, there would be no thing in her way.

In her turret, the damage was crazy. She began picking at and piling up branches, but was soon fatigued and scratched. Zap had triaged the ceiling but snow and cold still found their way in. She was ready to call a renovation company, a true renovator, when she remembered it was Sunday and all good men took their rest. She would resist calling that Aunt kidnapper to come inside her fortress. Anna continued to pile up branches. Some were intricately woven together, sculpted into organic architecture. She kept Feed Me for the day, since the cat seemed to enjoy those houses. Also she didn't want to have any contact with his owner.

By mid-afternoon the house looked no better. She hadn't thought where she'd put the branches, so they piled up near the top of the stairs. Each time she moved branches some bits and bark stayed behind on the floor, so her work was doubled. When the phone rang she was happy for the interruption.

We are so grateful, said the Director of Pearl's home. Often people don't listen to our advice, they think they know everything, when each of us faces elderly family for the first time. Anna thanked her back, said it was nothing. Which was true. She'd only spoken on the phone. She hadn't even talked to the police yet about the kidnapper, and…

"You're so cute, you two. 'Kidnapper.' Did he kidnap your heart too?"

Anna began to reiterate that the man wasn't her husband, but the Director insisted on thanking her again for sending him, because since that time Pearl had a new energy for her days. There's nothing like family, she said, to bring back a zest for life. She looks like she'll live forever! The idea of taking her out in the snowfall, and getting her to taste again what life is like out in the world—exactly what she needed.

Anna said she was so glad. She would come by as soon as her schedule was free. Yes, she would be sure to tell the husband what a hero he was.

Anna's jaw was misaligned. Her jaw malfunctioned before, when exams skewed her perspective, doctorates stretched her nerves. Misalignment was an occupational hazard. Her whole career, whatever sense she made of life hinged on the difference between the true and the forged. But Anna was trained to spot legend. It ran on synthetic oils. In history, there were no clear motives. Great Men were slippery. So now, surrounded by duplicity, her teeth didn't touch.

She knew she ignored the lie of her own romance novel. She understood this.

———

They don't align, Zap said. These joists and studs. He was up on the ladder, changed into white T-shirt and clean jeans for Anna. As much of a costume as anything else, he figured. Feed Me purred on the penultimate step like a lovely assistant.

Zap put him on his shoulder and brought him down. "Your cat sure is friendly. You stay down Rochester."

"What did you call him? I thought he was Feed Me."

"You call him that, I thought you liked it. Names don't matter to him. The tag is just instructions for people who find him."

"He's not your cat?"

She warmed to him, he could see that. The Pearl manoeuvre paid off, as he knew it would. And she couldn't turn to anyone else for the roof. Maybe he'd pushed a little far with the husband thing, but uttered words were magic. Something those in the writing business didn't always understand.

"Listen, I'll give you the job, but there's a few ground rules."

"Shoot."

"No calling yourself my husband."

"No husband," he said. He'd try to repeat the word as often as possible.

"Like I said before, respect my personal space."

He nodded. Personal was a good word too.

He rained down uttered words. Usually the kinds of words he liked and admired, not ones used to hide behind stone walls of obfuscation (he threw that one in free, for her). And speaking of stone walls, did she know the Moors introduced stone castles to a wooden Europe, because of the lack of timber in North Africa, and Spain provides most of the world's roofing slate, and what about that spaghetti sauce you had on the stove, and he may as well stay and stir, not that he's a *husband* or anything, no worries.

There's family, he said, stressed the word while they ate spaghetti at her table, a brother, Wolf Zaporzan up in the Laurentians built hunting outposts and ski huts, a sister Skye Zap who was a psychic and inner child babysitter, and a whole Slavic goulash of backyard distillers and trustworthy used car salesmen that culminated in this species of beast you see before you, do you have any fresh Parmesan?

Anna poked her head in the turret and breathed in the smell of cut wood. Zap behaved himself, and her bruise turned from purple to light green, her thoughts of Christophe from obsessed to incidental. In the evening the carpenter went to the other side of the brick wall, but when peace finally descended on the house she sat in front of her laptop and stared. That inventiveness of Zap, that was supposed to pour out of her too now. She needed potency in her teaching, in her romance novel. In her life. With all she'd crafted over the years she should concoct one Harlequin per coffee break. Write the whole romance on her phone in a doctor's waiting room. Hell, she could spray-paint it on the structural supports of the ramshackle Turcot Interchange if it came to that, with all the other lovesick vandals. But in the half-finished turret, among the sawdust, nothing came.

One last look before night. Zap rebuilt the ceiling so you wouldn't know. His work was joyful deception. He told lies to buildings, whispered to them true and real and they swooned under his touch. He had no interest in new. Like the cat, again on the ladder. A stray. Who knew what else was a lie. Family. Education. Pedigree.

She found a happy medium of half listening to him. He talked while he worked, like others whistled. Built stories. A new tool in his hand could inspire a tangent. His stories weren't the usual carpenter chatter you could ignore. He crafted stories about one thing and led to another. Turret design was excellent for shooting arrows along the castle wall, for instance. That led to a one-hour debate about the best advances in twelfth-century castle building, which Zap knew a surprising amount about, and then to the underestimated role of women in castle and bailey design, of which he was unaware, and Anna raised her voice and touched his shoulder once and Zap's back muscles twitched.

Zap had rebuilt machines and buildings and clocks with his father Petro. To remake the past was not the idea. To pay homage was. Hadn't studied anything. Not like her. He'd read books, he had to admit. He'd toured the heritage buildings of the city. Seen some stuff in the British Isles, also learned to drink there. Not self-taught—didn't believe that was ever true, since everybody had a hand in his education.

So now he used all modern conveniences to make things like new, the best devices the latest theories, and yet carried tools and ancient methods like relics. A great wooden hammer spilled from his toolbox, useful for stubborn emergencies, and he wielded a knife wrought from iron mine castoffs. She watched him work and remembered her father tinkering with noble materials in the garage. Not always sure of the technique, but of the intent.

At her university office she tried to channel Zap's creativity. A no trespassing sign for students hung on her door: History in the Making. But all she managed to create anew was a bilingual version of her sign: *À la recherche de choses perdues*. She left tasks unfinished, students agitated. Soon it would be Easter and exams and her performance review would rear its slimy head, but it was useless to look for creativity here. She shuffled through the snow back to her redoubt. What was she building?

> We rode under a ghost moon. Even in the waning day it threatened to pour out its powers on the barren hills. I didn't know where he was taking me, but if I didn't cling to him I'd be in the sand. We took hidden pathways that he unveiled. I tried to ask him where we were going, but had only learned a few borrowed words from the scholarly tongue of the Arabs and they only were able to communicate with hand signals. When we

stopped he conjured dates and almonds. I gingerly reached for his robe and pulled it aside to see how the wound was healing. The scar was too fresh for this travel, and still pulled apart at places. I disappeared for minutes, came back with my habit pockets filled with herbs and plants to lay on his chest. The first time I tried it he grabbed my wrist, and my balms fell on the ground.

The Dean opened her door to Christophe, gushed how she loved his approach, how his work on troubadours brought a new energy into her department, and how she envisioned, perhaps this spring, a concert of troubadours. That was all well, but Christophe had something more ambitious in mind. And Christophe sat down with her and over wine they talked of the job of Dean and how you were hated and loved, and how university politics were like tournaments and jousting, a long process of selecting the knights. Christophe offered that in those days, if knights lost the competition they lost their horse and armour as well, and destitute and hopeless often committed suicide. But there was another way, he looked in her eyes and through his wine, and that was the war game was love. Even in those brutish times, there were ways of moving up that were refined – poetry raised the lady of the court to heaven alongside the newly minted Virgin, it flattered her above her station. And grateful for a reason to live she brings the poet into the court. Romance rises as an alternative to sport—or death.

He cannot see himself embracing the Dean, who keeps close to her husband in the American way. He could, if he had to, but he preferred not to. There were less egregious methods. She is not swayed that way like the students, or assistant professors.

The troubadour concert, he says, is exactly what I'm talking about. On the grounds in the front of the traffic, the students, the office workers—this is what could reach out to the community around us. Because it is all about benefitting the students, he said, and if the reputation and visibility of the university grows and funding grows because of that, so much the better. But we cannot transform the university, we cannot transform Montreal, the world, without acknowledging history. We must encompass all around us, *la Grande McGill*. For as the greatest writer said: Truly innovative art is in the search of things past.

The Dean was easier to reach than he imagined. Impressed with language and accent and fine tailoring. With reaching out. She was ambitious herself, ambitious enough to imagine herself out of the Dean's position, entering the tournament of politics in the grand world beyond. Which suited Christophe fine. The sooner she moved on the better. She loved the idea, *la Grande McGill*; she knew very well of Christophe's work on *le Grand Paris* with the President of the Republic, and who better to organize it and fill a committee with the appropriate people, only she had her agenda full now, and till the end of the year, but could he draw something up?

Christophe needed Professor Hill. She would be his right hand, she knew the workings of Quebec politics, McGill, she looked perfect beside him, not taking the spotlight, only accentuating his lines, his suits (they would have to shop for her, tone her down, class her up). She would distract, and together they would show Paris how it was done, Paris would regret kicking him out to the colonies, Christophe would once more be a man.

Anna, in her comfortable robe and wool socks, took her work to bed. But she kept drifting towards her romance instead. She was a spy, decoding. She headed somewhere, but like her nun she lacked a divining compass. They had abandoned their convents. They looked for truths, and searched where they could, in the dark corners of the middle of the night, in fluorescent classrooms. In essays, in chick lit. Anna summoned the Moor and nun to her bed.

"If you don't trust me to help you I won't," I said. "You can die out here for all I care."

He didn't let go of my arm until I shook myself loose. I kept my chin up and my eyes on the distant hills. I got up and walked toward those hills by myself and left the brute to wither alone with his pride by these rocks. But I was back before sundown, because death and danger came quickly there. For the first time, I longed for the walls of the cloister, was nostalgic about the chores I did every day. I turned from the Moor and began my prayers, fondled my rosary. His figure a dark shadow out of the corner of my eye. I would scratch his eyes out with the cross if he grabbed me like that again.

A deep rumble came from his robes, his words a stew of resentment. I heard snapping and clicks, and soon a small fire blazed in the space between us. A rabbit roasted above it.

Eyes closed, jaw unaligned. The streetlight sparkles through the frost on the inside of her lids. She opens them and sees snowdrifts of exam papers on the floor around her. All that thirst for knowledge. All those past lives. What do they want from her? She pulls a random paper off the pile. Not at all random: a student proves romance's Arab origins with quotes from mystical love poems of Sufis in Andalusia. Her eyelids fall hypnotized again as she reads of the concept of conceptualizationing an entangled post-reflexivity as a generative methodological move in post-intentional gender specificity:

> My heart can take on any form: a meadow for gazelles, a cloister for monks. For the idols, sacred ground, Ka'ba for the circling pilgrim, the tables of the Torah, the scrolls of the Qur'án. I profess the religion of love; wherever its caravan turns along the way, that is the belief, the faith I keep.

By the last lines Anna has quit this world on a flying magical thinking carpet, peopled with Xs and Ys, carpenters and academics, fallacies and entanglements, knights and natives and Moors.

17. Black Ice

"Your hemoglobins," Dmitri says, tapping the side of his head. "Breaking down. Good thing." Anna knows her bruise shows yellow. These are the final stages, Dmitri tells her.

The wind blows through her jacket and sweater, pierces her skin and muscles, flows through her bones and out the other side. On the sidewalk in front of the Arts Building it is too frigid to think, but for Dmitri the wind is a spring breeze.

She breathes deep and lines her throat with ice. She has eaten only rice crackers today, she slept only a few hours last night. All she wants is to get out of this cold, out of her problems, past her performance review. Dmitri appears to want to offer help, but he stands in front of her, his bulk blocking some of the wind. She has heard his stories, as a Chair, of academic breakdown. It happens to women, he said, to men, even to Russians.

Anna stares at the Arts Building, a cupola atop it like a turret. The entrance columns want to speak of knowledge and security, but all Anna hears in the winter is their groans under a slippery weight.

Dmitri sneezes and unleashes a cloud of black pepper, and Anna flees for the protection of the grey walls.

><

Audrey shows up on time for her office hours. She plunges into students' problems and surfaces with what she believes are handfuls of treasure, her glasses askew and grin contagious. Audrey knows style and boys and how to play Renaissance madrigals on a sackbut. But she says nothing when Professor Hill arrives with a yellow bruise shining through her make-up. She stares at it instead.

"You should see the other guy," her professor jokes.

"Are we all right?" Audrey says.

"Our goblins are breaking down. Our performance is under scrutiny. The ice age is upon us. Otherwise, yes, we're all right. You?"

Audrey says she is sorry. And that Christophe—sorry again, she means Professor Auguste de Latour—has left a message for her, something about molding the past of the university to shape its future, *la Grande McGill*. Audrey looks up from her computer when the professor doesn't respond.

"Did you talk to him?" Anna says.

"He wants to see you outside the university."

Anna smiles. Audrey isn't convinced she's glad. Audrey messes her hair with one hand. She attracts men even as she does everything she can to make herself fade into the scenery: her geek glasses, her formless dresses, her shocking forgetfulness with makeup.

"Such a charmer," Anna says. She touches her bruise.

Jackson Zaporzan in her turret says, what's it like to always work in the past? Is it like time travel?

"You tell me. You're the one conserving old buildings."

"Huh. But I'm improving on the past."

"Me too."

Zap spreads plaster over drywall joints. He brags that he saved the original window. A little structural integrity.

"What did you want to be when you grew up?" he asks.

"You mean like a princess or a vet?"

"Is that what you wanted?"

"We all did. Didn't we?"

"Maybe a romance novelist?"

"Cowgirl. Nurse. Architect," Anna says quickly.

"Not a history professor."

"God no." She hasn't thought of her architect phase for years.

Anna once believed architecture had answers. Blueprints and expected outcomes. But her father said architects didn't have any more order or fewer surprises than the rest of us. If she wanted that, she could be a schoolteacher and reap a good pension at the end of it all.

If the boredom didn't kill her first, Dotty said.

Teaching is safe and solid and thrilling. He should know. You don't have to teach flying, mind you. You'll get summers off.

Dotty settled into her chair with a paperback. The best teacher, she said, is the one who won't tell you anything.

Don't listen to your mother, Edward said. The hippies got to her.

Anna flew to higher education. She thought herself a rebel when she targeted history. She would find context amid chaos.

That was the answer to her problems. In the past.

But now, in the glorious present, there's no job security. There's no guarantee that the thing they hired you for—your mind—would always be around. Does anyone even believe in history anymore?

18. Pleasures of the Flesh

On a day that looked like spring Anna opened the window to air the turret of wood and plaster and man. Halfway up it balked. The walls askew, or the frame too new, or the carpenter had hammered something backwards. Despite the south wind, the afternoon returned to winter.

All day the window refused. The turret frosted. Anna slowed down the damage with a garbage bag and towels. When she needed Zap, when he would be *useful*, he vanished. She thought: I am not surprised. She thought: disappointed. She rubbed her temple, moved her jaw, curled her toes. Every day the carpenter had filled the turret, one constant in a slippery equation. Not today. Feed Me cleaned his paws.

His truck wasn't out front. Unopened cans of paint in the turret, and paintbrushes wrapped in plastic. She looked at the texts he'd sent and started to write but erased her words. Didn't want him to think that... Didn't want to encourage him. Then she'd never get rid of him.

All she wanted was this room of her own to be complete. And then everything would be complete.

The only reason she could imagine him missing a day was someone in the hospital. Zap himself in the hospital, bandages and tubes and small beeps. Nurses wipe his eyes. In a coma. Hasn't carried ID, typical. Or worse, false ID. They give him something he's allergic to. Who would know? Or someone he's conned in the past exacts revenge. His jaw breaks underneath a baseball bat, unable to speak who he is. Yellow around the eyes, swollen cheeks, unrecognizable even to himself.

Anna was discomforted. She liked the word, the sound, the English countryside it evoked. She hated the feeling. Open to the winter like that. Walk around your own house in blanket and wool socks morning and night. She took epic baths. Conquered a box of Kleenex. Her breath was short and her legs weak. Dmitri said stay home. Three times a day her toes refroze. She would die alone and unremembered in this house. Like her Aunt Pearl, cobwebbed, mumbling inanities about love and loss.

Anna pretended she'd lost track of days. If this was forward or that was backward. And forget History, with a sock puppet head and popsicle toes. And the breath—she could see it—the breath came stunted, her lungs shrunk, her throat bitter. Okay, she wasn't asthmatic. But a hell of a cold.

The socks and television didn't help. No one brought her soup. She made her own, one hand on the counter, holding her phone. Bleeps and chimes like hospital monitors, but not the right people. Until the last time it rang she almost threw it in the pot with all the other nutrients, but saw the screen vibrate with faith, hope, charity, and answered with a voice choked and underused.

Christophe didn't recognize her voice. He wouldn't, she agreed. Crises and viruses did that.

You can't do everything by yourself, Christophe said.

Always have, she said.

We will stop this. I will come now. I have a proposition.

Now, Anna said, inside herself. You must tell him. He is too rough. He takes your body like your heart. When she needs a doctor's hands, a medic, a shaman. Both her hands gripped the counter. He should leave her. Alone. He should never.

"I made too much soup."

He would be right there.

"Can you bring fresh basil?"

Anna chose a big bowl the colour of cream. The fine vegetables were chopped to match the beans so that when the spoon came to mouth it would contain the herbed Tuscan sunshine of the field (no, she'd never been there). She chose the ladle with the organic curve on the handle. Potatoes crumbled on the tongue, carrots with the slightest crunch, the way each pea surrendered with a pop, the smoothness of the little pasta tubes filled with the juice of tomatoes, and a gentle but insistent background of bacon suffused with the smoke of farmers burning their fields in autumn (no, nor Provence in the fall). And when his bowl was filled almost to the top, she cradled the mix of parmesan and garlic and sprinkled that rawness of the Italian sun over the bounty of the land, and carried the bowl with two burning hands to set in front of Christophe.

He picked up his spoon and slurped. Then made faces as it burned his hard palate.

"You're not eating?"

"Not so hungry. It should really have basil."

"You could have asked me to bring some."

She said she had, but that was all right.

He said she never did, and Anna thought about it and perhaps she'd only thought of asking him, she was feeling lightheaded and not one hundred percent, but she didn't want to complain.

"You look pale," he said. "Maybe you could skip a meal or two."

Anna laughed and made a mental note to go heavier on the foundation and ease up on the starches.

"Did you see Audrey?" she asked. "She told me you had a message for me. The proposition?"

"How would I know where Audrey is?"

He filled his mouth with wine and pink steam bellowed out. He shook his head but could not speak, not yet.

"I wondered. I thought."

"You should be able to keep track of your assistant, at least."

"Oh Audrey, she's a loose cannon."

"You need help, it's obvious to everyone. That is why I'm here. I have the offer of security. To help you keep your tenure track."

He kept slurping the minestrone, and with each spoon he made more noises of protest at its heat. Anna made herself a cupful of the soup, sucked on pasta tubes.

"I will tell you the secret. I came here to transform McGill."

"And you thought you'd begin with my class?"

"The soup is good. Maybe you should have been a chef…"

"Thank you."

"…instead of a professor. The Dean hired me for this."

"For me?"

"For *la Grande McGill*. It is my concept. It is the university, transformed, inclusive, a new global future for all."

Anna had heard of *le Grand Paris*, all the university had. The former French president's plan to include the surroundings of the city through iconic projects. He'd assembled a huge committee made of architects, geographers, philosophers (this was France), historians. Christophe's invitation as consultant to that committee had won him this invitation to Montreal, an academic superstar. And now the Dean, and the Chancellor of course, were ready to reveal their plans to bring the outside world into the new *Grande McGill*, a university for the 21st century, guided by the knowing hand of Christophe.

"You're an adequate professor," he said, "and you would be better if you weren't so concerned only about your students. You will join me on my advisory committee."

"I don't think I could find time."

"If you don't, you may not be given more time to teach either."

Anna asked if he'd spoke to the Dean about her, but he only said that it would be better if she minded what she wore more often, something along classic lines, black suits for instance. The clothes were also more forgiving. Perhaps she would be better suited to the administration side? This committee will transform McGill, he said, it will change Montreal, the province, the country. It would be better to dress for posterity.

She followed the trail of soup around his bowl, up his shirt front, to the corners of his mouth. A leaf of parsley hid in his moustache. She reached her hand to his mouth.

He jerked his face away from her hand as if she'd slapped him. He looked around as if to see that others hadn't seen. "Don't ever do that," he said. But he held up his bowl when the minestrone was gone.

"*Dis donc*," he said, "when you would join, you could help me even more. Make it convenient for me to stay in the country."

"The basil," Anna said. "It really missed basil."

Christophe curled his fingers and tugged, but nothing gave, nothing fell. He put them in front of his face. The stuck window was a trick.

A test. He grimaced. Focused on the ceiling while he tried again. The window would not budge for him either. He turned.

"I cannot stay the night."

"No."

But he would not fail this test.

He moaned against the window. He wouldn't leave the window like that. No man could. Even a professor of medieval studies. Because what if the missing carpenter turned up. In time to see Christophe at the window, his brow freckled with sweat and his lips awash with curses, incantations and grunts. The window began to squeak and fight its nature. A centimetre. Another. Until with a great protest it loosed from the frame, screamed mercy and pity, and Christophe let it plummet with the finality of a guillotine.

His hands shook. One trembled across his forehead, and he intoned a litany of Gallic obscenities. Anna stepped back to the doorway.

"*Merci*," she whispered.

Christophe whirled around, a sneer sliced across his face. He looked down at his hands for a second, then he kicked his leg through the air and the heel of his black lace-ups shattered the glass.

Anna froze.

He bent over, filled his lungs like a marathoner. Nobody moved. Anna's eyes watered. She blamed her sinuses, the north wind. Christophe finally straightened and let out a cold breath. The frost held her to the floor by her toes, even though her heart beat faster and her body was warm inside, even when he took a step towards her and gripped her shoulder.

She kissed him, and he froze. Then his fingers found her hair and before he could think he pulled back her head again, and spun her around against the broken window. "The window was already cracked," he said. He covered her mouth, and let the cold wind blow across them. His other hand slid underneath her blouse, then into her pants. Anna's stuffed nose struggled to breathe. They stood among the broken glass, the edges along the frame scratching Anna's arms, drawing blood from Christophe's hand.

"You like it," he whispered close to her ear. "I can feel you wet inside. You're a bad girl."

She bit his hand, and he drew it back quickly, cut it further on the glass. "*Putain*." He looked at his hand for a second, then drew it across the front of Anna's neck. He turned her around to face him, and licked his own tinny blood. They were on the floor, and he made love to her that she would never forget.

"To hell with your body," he said. "I want your soul."

But he didn't say that. Anna recognized the melodramatic language. Those were the words of the FalconMoor.

> He lay lit by moonlight in the sand, his belly full of rabbit. His eyes finally closed, at least one need sated. So deeply did he sleep that it was nothing for me to pull his thin curved scimitar from its leather sheath. I sawed through the rope around my ankle in two thrusts. I was free. I gripped the leather hilt with both hands and felt its weight. And now, as I held it above my head with two hands as if in prayer, the Damascus steel gleamed in the moonlight. I intoned an ancient prayer, and just as the Moor's eyes opened when the reflected light hit his face, I swung the blade at his throat and sliced it open. When it hit bone I let go. It stayed in his neck, vibrating. Blood flooded the

dry desert floor. Then I was on his horse, and rode into the great nothingness.

Oops. That wouldn't work.

I sawed through the rope around my ankle in two thrusts. I was free. With an infinite quiet I slipped the saddle on the Andalusian Arabian horse. The leather creaked and the horse protested, and I had trouble putting the bit in its mouth. I gathered my skirts and climbed astride the beast like a man. Then I was off, still holding the scimitar with one hand and clinging on for life with the other. We galloped into the night and collapsed in the morning by a deserted shepherd's shack on a hill.

I dreamed of being ravaged, and it woke me up. It made me angry because the Moor hadn't mishandled me once. Of course I saw how he looked at me. His eyes between the fabric of his turban were dark and filled with passion. He may only have stopped himself because of his arm. It took two arms to hold a woman like me. In the morning I woke up, my habit disheveled and my hair spilled on the rocks, loosed from prisons. But it was only my own restless sleep that had done it.

Although I was tired and exhausted, I struggled back on the horse. "You'll take me home," I said. Wherever that was. I was a nun covered in grime and dust and smelled like a horse, and my habit was wet with the beast's sweat. My legs and bottom swelled with sores.

"First of all," Julia said from the other side of the pond, "you can't have no dolly with crotch rot."

Anna had phoned Julia in a small panic. Her hero kept dying at the hands of the nun.

"It's called fantasy," said Julia. "Play-time. You don't want your girls putting down the book to finish the laundry. So we don't want any smells or funny tastes down there. Keep it in the 'moist petals' range, or the warm damp dark haven, or better yet something sweet and desperate, like a lava cake, but don't use that."

"Okay," Anna said, "but I'm more worried about something else. Is he too dangerous? Maybe readers don't want that. If this is escapism, maybe that's the first thing they want to escape."

"Oh they want bad. That's not the problem. They want daring and confident and incorrigible. Which is horsefeathers, because probably you're not going to get that in your life, and if you do you're going to drop the dope. What is different from life, is that in our romances he's going to change. He's got to. He's going from cad to dad. Turns out, he was in love all this time and didn't want to show it. And you get the best of both worlds. That's what we want to read. You don't hurt your real hubby, and you won't get no bun in the oven from some dirty baker, but you can live out your cinnamon fantasy and keep your petals moist."

"I guess."

"You all right? Still seeing your professor?"

Anna wanted to say more. She wanted to ask questions into the night, which came sooner in England, and she wanted to talk like Julia and let things roll off her back and into the pond.

"He likes my cooking."

"I bet."

"So I keep being bad?"

"You're doing the opposite of reality. Freedom. Joy. Those are your safe words."

"I don't…"

"Research, girl. Boldly go. But stay away from the cads in real time."

I, Angeles the nun, clung to the horse's mane. It was coarse and long and blew in my face. It smelled like the FalconMoor too, the ointments and salves on his body. I was rocked to sleep by the movement of the Arabian's powerful shoulders as the horse climbed hills and descended into valleys. The horse kept to the meagre trees, instinctually wary of the Christian arrows. When the horse found a pool of water he dipped his head. I slipped off and, on my hands and knees, drank from the pool too. Then I peeled off my clothes and leapt into the water. The horse watched me, then tried a few tentative hooves as well. We floated and drank and forgot we had nothing to eat. The Spanish sun sought us out. But I knew we had nowhere to go. I threw away some of my filthy clothes and my apron and rinsed others and fashioned myself a new habit. It would have been scandalous in the nunnery, or at the gates of a town, but here there was no one to comment. And like that, freer to move, unencumbered by so much cloth, I once more climbed onto the horse. I felt him this time, felt the movements of each leg, felt how he felt me. And like that, the horse went where I wanted. From the unforgiving sky came a scream. High above the mountains, a falcon circled, descending in tighter and tighter arcs.

Anna was on a rescue mission, is what she told herself. Her car parked under a cocoon of snow, she decided to hoof it (in Julia's lingo). She imitated her nun too, off on adventures through the semi-arid plateaus. Assertive. Riding to her destiny. No dunes were available outside. But there was snow enough for a Russian tragedy.

She was off to save Auntie Pearl. She still had never met the woman, but the reports coming from La Falaise Manor for Assisted

Living were disconcerting. Pearl was not behaving as an eighty-six-year-old woman missing one leg and a breast should behave. For one thing, she was dancing. She had been spotted in the Manor's gym on a treadmill. Staff found her before she figured out how to turn it on, but still. She explained she was training for the upcoming dance. Dotty told Anna that there was no such thing as a dance at La Falaise. She'd also tried more exit-seeking, including one memorable time when she was disguised as a man in a floppy-eared hat with yellow sunglasses.

Anna told her mother not to worry, she'd go see Pearl and straighten things out. Dotty wondered if they should invite her to Easter next week, but Anna said she wasn't sure if she was comfortable with that.

The snow blew across the sidewalk in a thin mercury wind. Anna was not comfortable with many things, including the matching ski underwear she had on. She'd bought it after that last encounter with an ecosystem. The material was high-tech and made of a kryptonite and yeti hair blend, but it was so tight it rubbed on the multiple bandages on her arms and chaffed between her legs.

Which reminded her of the other discomfort.

She'd taken Julia's advice, and started research on sado-masochism. It was fine while she looked at pictures about spanking and even hot wax, but with her typical academic fervor she couldn't stop there, and when she got into the details about breast clamps and Saint Andrew's cross and suspension slings she started to squirm. Which made her more uncomfortable.

But she didn't take long to see the whole BDSM thing was about something she hadn't yet broached with Christophe. Whatever anyone got from it, or why they did it, it all revolved around consent.

These people negotiated; they trusted each other. They did something called *aftercare*.

That word lodged in her head, and now on the way to see Pearl it mixed squeamishly with any kind of special care her aunt might get. All that research was still saved on her phone. Very soon Anna lost her enthusiasm for her rescue mission, and she stopped cold on Avenue des Pins with a scrunched up look on her face.

And because of that word, she decided right there to take control of her own destiny, and let other people take care of their destinies. She was ready to negotiate. To trust. To get herself some aftercare. Even if that meant she first had to negotiate a bare-bottomed spanking.

The sidewalk snowplow rattles by and leaves a slick surface. Anna's boots are oiled suede lined with alpaca wool, sealed with the bleeding hearts of seal mothers. They are new with the underwear, but comfortable for her sensitive toes. Even her purse is lined with downy fluff. Or maybe it's acrylic. Her phone is warm inside.

She skates up the stairs to Christophe's condo, then stops. Could she find all the research again? She should have printed it out, with argument, citations, a few stats. She had an idea for a chart too, but didn't print it. The stats alone were impressive: fifty-three percent of male sadomasochists develop an interest in the sport before the age of fifteen. Seventy-eight percent of women SMs embrace it *after* fifteen. But now at his door even the stats aren't relevant. They sound like they're pulled from that popular bondage trilogy. She does not have a gift wrapped in Japanese paper with hemp rope and a suggestion of musk. She cannot lay down her heart on the threshold.

A Nordic skier schusses down the far sidewalk. Anna turns back to the door and takes off one glove. She does not have appropriate underwear for this. It covers ninety percent of her body.

The pricey lingerie isn't the problem. She is ready to admit she may have control issues. She should have stayed at home. She tried. She opened The FalconMoor and saw no way to happily ever after. She doesn't want so many stories in her life. She wants to cut down narrative threads like soldiers at the Battle of Poitiers: one king, one queen, one god.

Her fingers freeze while she doesn't knock. When she peers through the stained-glass windows around the door she notes they are Gothic Revival. A shadow moves inside, and she ducks behind the door. Breathe. You are a tree. From the roots, to the leaves, exhale to the universe. She knocks.

A lock unbolts. A mop of black hair shakes, then underneath it a woman's distrustful eyebrows. Anna tries to bring in buckets of subzero air but her trachea is coated with ice.

Christophe laughed for a long time, long after the cleaning lady had left, after Anna had tried to give her a generous tip and apologized for screaming at her. She's suffered worse than that, the cleaning lady said. She was Polish. Her accent was thick, her hair black despite her age.

"To see you dancing like that on my front porch," Christophe said. "And for her. You must think me desperate." He'd watched the confrontation from the sidewalk. He still sat in his ski clothes on the porch. They sat on a lime-green bench. Anna wanted to go home. "Would you stop checking your watch for a second?"

"This is a heart-rate monitor." The pants and jacket and hat were all tight-fitting and different from the gear she'd seen before and he had new awful sunglasses on his head too.

"I'm glad I bumped into you," she said.

"You bumped into my cleaning lady."

"It's an expression."

"Tell her that."

Anna sat down. She wished he would stop laughing and kiss her. He checked his monitor. Maybe she should have printed out that chart. She reached inside her purse and fondled her phone.

"I need to clarify a few points. First we need trust if we're going to go further. We should each reveal something about ourselves."

"Okay, I'll reveal I thought a *sans-abri* was at my door."

"My point. You ignore me in public. First you kiss my collarbones and tear my lingerie and now I don't know if you're psycho or kinko." Anna realized she stood again, her back to the door. She'd said it. Not like she planned. Not with the research logic.

"You can't tell who anyone is in all that winter fluff. I thought I should call the police," he said, still chuckling, "but I don't know the number in Canada."

"Nine-one-one."

"Not one-one-two?"

Anna sighed. "This isn't how it's done," she said. "There are rules."

"I think if each continent has its numbers…"

"You know what I mean."

He unzipped his collar. "You have a system."

"Because if there are no rules in place then games become abuse."

Christophe looked up at her. From this perspective, his eyes looked dark and hooded. Wrinkled. Old. She stood at the door, her purse a shield.

"You invent words. 'Kinko' is not real."

"I mean, maybe I love you, but who chokes someone on the first date?"

Christophe looked at his heart monitor. Something was wrong with it. He shook it. "These numbers are not correct. Digital is no good."

"It's a paraphilia, not a mental disorder. I looked it up. Fifty-three percent of male…"

"Love."

"Hmm?"

"Love is a paraphilia. A fetish." He stood up, unzipped his jacket, began to shed his layers. "Because love, love is self-gratification. You do not relate to me. You glorify yourself."

He didn't smell like himself, like spilled Bordeaux, or cologne, or *crêpes au Nutella* beside the Seine. He smelled like heated polyester, wet GoreTex, ski wax. She could smell this perfectly, because he stood inches from her and tapped his finger on her breastbone.

"Come inside," he said. She did.

"Really you have come to tell me you will join *la Grande McGill* committee. The Dean, the Chair, they're not on your side. They're lying to you if they say that. The only one on your side is me. Close the door."

The moment she closed it he threw her against the wall. He pushed her to her knees and held her hair. "Suck me," he said. He struggled to pull down his tights with the other hand, and thrust himself in her face. "You see that. You see that I am hard for you. That means one thing." He put it in her mouth. "That you are the only one for…"

Anna pushed him away with a strength she didn't know she had. She pushed him in the balls, and it sent him back and doubled over.

She wiped her mouth and stood. Sounds like crying came out of him. She put her hand on his shoulder. He stood up and laughed.

"You think that was SM, that was rough? That was lust. The same as love, in the end."

Anna searched for the doorknob behind her.

"You want me to be rough with you."

Anna didn't answer. Her hand was on the doorknob and Christophe's hand was on hers.

"It excites you."

His living room was beige of personality. Made for visiting professors to come, to go. She clutched at his finger on her breast. Bent it back. His expression didn't change. He had no expression. She looked in his eyes again.

"Don't threaten me. Rage does not match your outfit." Christophe stared at her. His head a quarter turn, his lips parted. After a while, after too long, he stepped back. He studied her red face, the wind not to blame.

"Marry me," he said. "I'm the only stable thing in your life. We'll play with your *rules*."

Part III:
Here Come the Sun King

19. Bunny

Easter weekend. Anna and Quince in light jackets, on the streets of the West Island. Anna's arm extends, jerks in front of her. Otto the pug has discovered road kill: a fluffy white bunny, neatly eviscerated. The job done by someone who knew what they were doing, or at least a car that knew where it was going.

"Does this mean the whole pagan festival thing is over?" Quince asks.

Otto insists. He dives in and squirms with delight. The kill is his now, the great hunter. Until he flies through the air, yanked by his leash. Anna screams at him. She loses control of the leash and he tumbles into the other curb, returns to his prey. More screams, more demands that he return.

"Gross," Quince says. "Now he's got guts in his ears."

Anna's fingers are numb. She fumbles with the leash but doesn't want to touch the dog and he doesn't want to be touched. In her dress she kneels beside the disaster in the reddened snow. Her hands on her face dig into her forehead, knead below her eyebrows. She is numb all over, except where she can't reach. All she wants is to lay down and sleep the sleep of the dead.

"Are you…" Quince begins, then thinks better of it. Anna's shoulders rise and sink. The sound of great breaths, obstructed by a late winter cold. Then the shoulders stutter. Quince looks around, scoops up Otto under one arm. "I got him," he says. "Come on."

After a few long minutes she lifts her head. Anna finds some clean snow and washes her face till it bites. "Bunnies, for god's sake," she says. "What is wrong with this neighbourhood?"

⋈

"Since when are you an animal lover?" Dotty asks. "And what kind of cat does that to your arms?" Quince rolls his eyes. Their mother produces a list of past infractions and accidents Anna committed against the animal kingdom, wild and domestic, all the way back to the number of turtles flushed and up to a beagle on Prozac.

Anna caresses her Band-Aids. Sure she's lost a few things on the way. Beginning with her father. All the fated pets. Boyfriends. Teaching assistants. And in the last weeks, all life support: her turret, her retreat, the carpenter who promised to make it whole. The support of the Dean and Chair, if Christophe is to be believed. Tenure, maybe even her job next year. All she has left is Christophe and his tousled hair, on the edge of a cliff fighting a stiff wind. He has thrown his phone into the sea. There is no answer.

She rummages through her purse for Advil and finds better: the ancient pillbox Dotty gave her with bits of Clonazepam. There is only a quarter left, a tease. She doesn't want to ask Dotty for more. She wipes at the blood on her pantyhose. Who could foresee an Easter Bunny assassin?

Quince and Dotty don't let her go, not yet. They get her out of the bedroom where she's been dialing Christophe's numbers on speakerphone over and over, listening to the ring like tinnitus. She knows it is wrong to do this at her mom's. Regression is futile. But he's turned off all his devices. A catastrophe. No one is unreachable anymore. In a proper movie the bunny would have foreshadowed this. Christophe has met with an Act of God. A minor one that involves kitchen knives or hot water, the kind that makes you temporarily, for a weekend, unable to glide fingers over a phone screen. Blood and screams in the condo that nobody can hear or understand, given the foreign accent, given the choice of exotic blasphemies, and no one knows he is a visiting professor and has been lying in a coma for three days while the life force ebbs from the ends of those digits and the only thing that he envisions in his final moments is Anna, always Anna, who waits for him at the altar with her answer, why did he ever want to be alone, where is Paris, where was

"Anna."

The lack of sleep kills her memory and alertness, she knows, eventually hallucinations and psychosis will set in, she's researched it. Not unlike the feeling she gets when she walks through Dotty's front door. This is not the state you want to be in when contemplating marriage. You want stability. You want a man with connections to the French presidents, with a summer house in Provence and a kindly caretaker named Gustave. Is that all she wants?

"Anna?" Dotty stares at her daughter's face. She is only six inches away. Everything else is dark.

"Give me a minute. I've almost got this worked out."

"It's midnight dear. You should go to bed." Quince left hours ago. She would stay a little longer. Until Wednesday, say. The time to decide one thing. Anything.

Something wanted in. Alone in her bed she heard scratches at the door. Or out. It wanted out. Out of its rabbit hole dark, humid and rank. Suffocating in there. Did rabbits have claws? But Anna knew she would die if she couldn't sleep, that the future of the civilized world depended on the next few hours, minutes, seconds—she burrowed into pillow feathers. Her dream stretched into gauze and threatened to disintegrate. She wanted back in. Into love.

>We nuns lay under the same night sky, but now my heart was as far from their commandments as my feet were from those cold stone walls. Because beside me under that Light lay the FalconMoor, who had tracked and recaptured me. But now he was mine. He avowed what no one before had dared. No priest. No commoner. And like the waves along the shores of the Great Civilizing Sea, his whispered heresies swelled my belly with desire.
>
>Above us the mourning dove cooed and the Moor's eyes overflowed like the discovery of a newborn spring. Those eyes languid and dark gazed upon my eyes, now discreet in their cloaks. His falcon too gazed upon them, unwise to the complications that grew between the Moor and me, how we could never hope to reciprocate each other's affections. The falcon cried out for our pain. The Moor joined. And his wails led to a song of longing and desire, and with his falcon tambourine he beat out a rhythm like that of his wounded heart. He sang of one soul broken in two, half of it deep in the heart of me, Angeles the nun, and the other filling the form of the desperate FalconMoor.
>
>It was the first romance and the only one in the world, and soon it would grow to spread like a benevolent plague through Al-Andalus and over the mountains and into all of Europe, but all those troubadours and knights of wooden spears would never equal his passion-love, whose certain cure lay in the next world…

On Day One Dotty pulled Otto from the bedroom door, but by Day Two she let him scratch claw and whimper. Anna didn't react anymore to bargains and prayers. Her ears tingled numb like the arms underneath her head. Red hair in a tangle, unwashed, uninhibited. She spent twenty-six hours without food, then two hours filling herself when her mother went out. All the greats were seduced by art on their beds: Proust, Colette, Joyce. Frida Kahlo, Brian Wilson, Tracey Emin. Protected from ills and drafts, horizontal, rested and safe. Naked before the gods, or robed in the kindest tissues. This is where the world began: conception, dreams, nightmares. All she needed was a few more hours. She would birth something. If it killed her. She would C-section it out. Her mother scratched at the door, a mad doctor. Throaty moans in reply, mixed with the complaints of the dog. No access.

What she couldn't do, and she only admitted the failure after feverish hours in the first evening, after tossed ideas and contraptions from head to paper to dream, what she couldn't do was teach classes from bed. The only solution was to be posthumous, postfamous, and incapacitated like Kahlo, but she wasn't; she wasn't even a celebrity scholar the world clamoured for dead or alive. Unlike others in her circle. Two days of classes passed, her phone never rang, and she let no one know of her inability to un-embed herself.

Beside the bed, hidden among the Kleenex and spillage of her purse, her phone lay gutted. The battery ripped out, thrown in a corner. In case paramedics broke in and fought to turn it on. In case anyone had open-heart surgery and tried to call. In case Anna needed mouth-to-mouth communication. The laptop too stayed buried in her bag until four-thirty in the morning, when she remembered her mother had no use for a wireless connection. Within minutes she added three life-giving paragraphs to the FalconMoor. A trinity she now believed could forever alter the nun's world, the Moor's destiny, could rescue Anna Hill of Coleridge Park. The sentences came to her in a dream, fully punctuated. In the labyrinth of the Nun and Moor's hearts beat the first blood of romance. Their child. They had no need of phones. Texts. Mere words.

Day Three. A tap dripped in the connected bathroom. The skin around her eyes stained wine barrels, her lenses streaked with Bordeaux. The pillbox still empty. If there were monsters at the door she no longer noticed. Anna lay on her back, unmoving, unmoved. Deep breaths, unbrushed teeth. She was ready to rise, but knew she would have to confront the mirror. Her pulse slow as a guru's. She could feel it under the pillow. Her body misunderstood hunger and midnight.

Day Four. "Honey?"

Day Five. New voices at the door. New sensations in her body. Sunlight through cracks in the blinds. "Professor Hill? It's Audrey?"

Anna made a sound. To her it sounded like a self-conscious animal. One with free will, and a good job. The person outside was not fooled.

"We're concerned. You're all over Twitter. Speculation is viral."

Anna cringed at the term. She didn't consider the effects of a downturn in evaluations. Nor did she recall at that moment the disdain her Teacher's Assistant had for doors, opened for chivalry, closed for business, separating the environment from its life forms. "I offered," Audrey said through the door, "to take your classes. But the Dean shut them down. What I do have is a bottle of Gewürztraminer if it doesn't interfere with medications, meant to be imbibed like *Le Déjeuner sur l'herbe* all bathed in light and scandal."

More animal sounds. The bedroom door inched open. Otto scurried through and began to clean around the bed. Audrey bit her lower lip when she saw Anna and the dark room. A cavern smell slid out the door. Audrey tried not to change her expression when Anna breathed on her.

"Did you sleep with him?" Anna said.

"Who?"

"Him."

"Are you crazy?" She might have phrased the question better. But no, she said. The reality was that Him looked at her funny one day and Audrey ran the other away to her mother's for Easter too, but earlier than planned, to uncomplicate things, avoid crucifixion, and now that Anna rolled back the stone and Audrey opened the blind and the window full as summer… it was… she would never… Audrey held Anna. Anna blubbered. Otto rolled on a pile of clothes and got trapped in a wool sock.

"People keep disappearing," Anna said.

20. Harassment Assessment

Despite his apprehensions about freedom protests and TA responsibilities and declarations of war on men, Dmitri sent the best person he could think of to find Anna.

Audrey discovered her professor locked in at her mother's house, and freed her, and encouraged therapy. Audrey said Anna should stop worrying if she'd slept with Christophe, and said if Professor Hill had anything to tell her she could. Anything at all.

"But she didn't want to talk," Audrey told Dmitri. "She only said there was a difference between passion and Vexatious Behaviour."

"Just and sufficient cause," Dmitri said, who unlike many boys and men preferred to keep Audrey at arm's length. "Form A-09."

"There are times for forms and legalities, but this is not that. You didn't smell her bedroom."

"Questions are raised. Digital questions. Her disappearance, bruises, the Visiting Professor."

"I know right? And if we let things go on, she's going to be screwed, not in the good way." Audrey touched Dmitri's hand. His phrases shortened when he was nervous. Audrey's did the opposite.

"It comes down to freedom, and freedom is loving yourself, which means you respect yourself, and others respect you, and that makes you responsible, and you stop being the victim, and make choices and your life is between your hands. Freedom." Her fist was in the air.

Dmitri said that liberty was a slippery and squidgy thing, and that his mother country was still trying to grasp it. But his responsibilities lay more in processing complaints, and he hoped Audrey could also encourage Anna to fill out a Form A14 (English) and see a Harassment Assessor. In the meantime, he would have an informal vodka with the Dean. And though Audrey was completely free to do as she pleased in this country, he asked her to please put on hold any public protests or civil disobedience she might have planned, as it could interfere with her academic career.

Nevertheless the rumours multiplied and grew. By the time Dmitri poured the drinks the Dean claimed to know more than he did about the Situation, and said that in her administration there was no way any visiting professor would get a chance to thrust his *Grande McGill* upon anyone. Before it even had a chance to reach tumescence, *la Grande McGill* lay flaccid and shrunken on the Dean's desk. By the end of the afternoon the program was completely cut off.

There was one thing missing, Anna decided. Yes, she would make an appointment with a therapist, a wonderful idea. Yes, she had some medication; Dotty, in a desperate bid to be a better mother, slipped her a few Clonazepam. Anna thought she would first go through the pills to see if things looked better that way, and then call the therapist. Audrey had filled her fridge with ready to eat gluten-free vegetarian dishes. Zap still hadn't come by, so Audrey had also cleaned up Anna's turret the best she could. So that was all good. And there was less frost on the window, and more streams of water in the streets. That wasn't it. What was missing, she thought as the first Clonazepam settled into her system and she looked down at her fingers, was that there had been a marriage proposal, but she hadn't seen a ring.

She breathed deeply, exhaled, and got up from her sofa with a grunt. She went to the turret, unhooked her satchel from the wall, and began at Page One:

> He saw me from across the room. His glance told me to stay where I was and not move. I couldn't anyway. He waved a necklace. I was unable to get out of the bed, and when I tried I limped and fell to the tiles.
>
> "I am the Falconer," he told me. His horse stayed where it was without a command.

She didn't recognize her heroine. And the Falconer should be holding a ring, not swinging a necklace around. Nothing was in focus. Literally. She felt her own heart, not figuratively. A falcon screamed down on her and she ducked. A muffled medieval peal of bells. She shifted and it grew clear and frantic.

Now would be a good time to call that therapist. Immediately. Anna dialed a number. It rang for a good while until a familiar voice answered and a face came on the small screen.

"Sex," said Anna. "I don't understand the language. I know a few words, some handy expressions. Enough to get myself into trouble, as they say. And it sounds like a beautiful language. I like the way sex sounds."

She was sure Julia would have answers, and cost less than a therapist. Also, they could talk about structural problems and forced sex in romance novels instead of some stranger asking her what brings you here.

"Too many dialects," Julia said. "Once upon a time, the hero raped the heroine. Aggression wasn't seen as a hate crime. He desired her, in the worst way." She was in her London office. "Passion though—savage, hungry, hell-bent—it's still legal in all states."

"Can I ask you something? As a romance editor?"

She crouched on the floor, spoke to the screen filled with Julia's bobbing head.

"All levels of sensuality are considered. And yes, there's heaps of sexy heroes in the halls of our office."

"I imagine."

"Imagine is what we do best."

"So no. What if a character says love isn't about the other person. Love is about yourself."

The connection crackled. Julia's face froze into pixels and melted again.

"Hello?"

"Intercontinental connections. Untrustworthy."

"Huh."

"Heart in mouth. Your characters love what they fear."

Julia disintegrated. Then Julia's voice said if Anna didn't e-mail her those love-simple characters tomorrow, she'd bill her for the time of this call and the rest of the time spent waiting for them.

Christophe strode down the slippery sidewalk, searched his pockets for his favourite antacid tablets. The bloom was definitely off the rose for these Canadian winters, as if a rose could even consider surviving here. Spring had arrived in name only and a suit jacket was no protection against the polar vortex. He rubbed his hands together, no gloves either, not even his preferred leather driving gloves. He walked with his head down, hoping a student would be stupid enough not to move out of the way for him, and he would at least be given the pleasure of upending someone's ass on the ice. Where were those tablets? He could feel the acid destroying the lining of his stomach.

He stopped at a streetlight, finally lifted his head. A student nearby recognized him and thought of approaching him, but then reconsidered when he saw the professor's scowl. Who were these people, out for blood. The Chair, the Dean—he thought he'd handily brought them to his side. Now they flung out innuendo and suggestion like so much confetti. Harassment! He'd told them what he thought of their Harassment Assessors, and their university, and their winters. He could probably sue them out of existence, if he had the first idea how that worked in this country. They assured him in their polite Canadian nothingness, that nothing was public, nothing was official, they just wanted to give him a chance to modify his behaviour. They assured him while they surrounded him with torches and pitchforks. Well he would modify. If they wanted a monster, he would give them a monster. He started with a low growl, which moved people on the sidewalk away from him. He lifted his face to the frigid sky and roared at the colonials.

But everybody in their northern politeness had left him alone.

He hadn't eaten today. Had rushed out to be on time to serve this twisted institution. Then forgot throughout the day, so absorbed was he in helping the students. He went into the nearest café. More students. He grunted in response to their greetings, asked for double of everything, including pastries. Sat in a corner to put it all away, tried to find warmth, cursed the Canadian ineptitude with *boulangeries*, the milky dependence of their lattes. As he glanced over his shoulders crumbs littered his jacket.

Each student that came in was a potential rat. A falsifying rat. He'd never abused anyone in his life. Women loved him. He worshipped them. Told the Dean as much, when she first started hinting at the rumours. The Dean with her small hands, her tiny mouth. Such dirty accusations out of those pouting lips. She had the body of a teen, undeveloped breasts and no hips. No wonder the children loved her, she was one of them, promoted to adult heights. Those heights that were his to scale and occupy. He couldn't believe they'd made her Dean of the Arts. Next they'd hire a woman as chancellor. Probably a former student. One of the students that had come to him with her problems, and when he was open and vulnerable, had seduced him. Like that TA. She appreciated his playful nature.

"Anything else, professor?"

He jerked his head up like a fish on a line.

In the Dean's office he'd thought he smelled alcohol. Not a reassuring trait. Should probably be pointed out to the Chancellor. That's why her accusations were so flimsy and vague. He walked over to her desk and sniffed. Looked for dirty glasses. She hadn't been able to name who he supposedly vexed. Was it students, he asked and sat down on the soft chair. He looked up at her, his big brown eyes. Because students drive what I do. We're not sure, said the Dean, if you have a solid understanding of McGill's mission. There's been some lapses in judgement. We hope you'll finish your contract, but if there's need for dismissal you have a concurrent right to due process.

"I've a concurrent right to kick your ass," he muttered. Who was she to screw with his career, the reputation he'd built up over the decades?

"Also, with reference to your career, it seems you never were actually hired to serve on the President's Advisory Board for *le Grand Paris*."

"My name was on top of the list."

"Apparently it was removed at some point. After similar lapses."

"This is not my fault. You must stick to the facts. As an academician, you know invention and imagination have no place in a university. Without facts you are nothing."

She had none, of course.

He was in possession of reality. In the café, he ordered one more latte and banana bread. He cursed the habit of overloading everything with cinnamon, as though it were the only spice in existence, as if these were the spice islands and… Anna. Anna and her imaginary worlds. He brought out his phone from his purse.

The usual onslaught of messages from her. Pages of rants, pleads, supplications. She wouldn't bring these false charges against him. They had an understanding. They were adults, in the privacy of… where ever. The next time she texted or called he'd answer, if he wasn't busy. A day had gone by without word from her. He looked for her on-line, and found no new postings. Just a charming photo from years ago, half the frame taken up by her hair. When the café door opened cold air blew in, followed by the smell of her hair. He closed his eyes. Her body, her lips. He could possess that reality too. He opened his eyes again, but it was just another student.

But that other lover, back in Paris. He thought he had control of her too, but she went her own way. He would not be careless again. Anna would stay by him, she would need him. If she stuck to her quaint hobbies, her inventions and imaginations. Talked to herself. Wrote a rosewater romance. Sure of nothing but him. Not even sure of her place in a university.

The hidden things. She hadn't told anyone about her romance novel. If that leaked out. From an anonymous student who couldn't wait for evaluations at the end of the course. Christophe looked around the café. Picked a student, and became her. Scribbled the note. On paper, and hoped it wouldn't be too obvious that no millennial student would write on something as passé as *paper*, slipped it in the Dean's mailbox. The note said: We revere Professor Anna Hill for her dedication to the students and this class, but with the time she puts into concocting and selling her romance novel outside of the university we fear she confuses her serious work with little nothings.

Without facts you were nothing.

21. Appropriate Risks

Anna Hill, at her door on the landing, breathing heavy. The letter still in her hand. Who still sent paper letters?

We regret to inform you.

The sun warmed the air today, but Anna shivered. She couldn't move.

"A downward trajectory."

The letter was impossible.

"Questionable significance."

They didn't understand.

"May lead to a new and potentially even more rewarding vocation."

Anna put her hand on the doorknob, not as cold as usual. But she couldn't close it, or open it further. Her palm was damp and slipped on the metal. When she tried to take her breath deep from the chakra, she found none. As if in opening the door she'd stepped into the void of space. Ripped the envelope open, ripped the fabric of the galaxy. Her galaxy, anyway. The end was here, under the feeble sun of spring.

I am a professor. I am nothing but a professor. I profess to be an expert in my field.

On the street people went on with their lives. Students laughed and made wet snowballs. People stuffed their hats and gloves into pockets. They still believed in possibility. But since Anna read the letter, all her possibilities ran from her.

The day had begun with hope and blue sky. A full night's sleep, or at least six hours, thanks to the pills. She smiled on waking. That had been awhile. She'd found a therapist, would call her today. Remembered Julia's gentle encouragement. Audrey's support. People who cared. And she did have a marriage proposal. Of a sort. Her future might not be all wine and romance, but it was headed in the right direction now.

And then she looked down the stairs and saw the envelope lying on top of flyers by the door. And in a short page, everything she worked for all her life was refused. That was how you were denied tenure.

Her breath came in shallow gasps. She coughed once, and then she couldn't stop, she would choke to death here on the landing, and they would find the letter in her hand. Her best revenge.

She was already down on one knee, dizzy. Someone called her name. A hand on her shoulder.

"Professor?"

She recognized Sanjay's shoes. He lifted her up.

"Should I call an ambulance?"

She would live. That would be better revenge. File an appeal. For the students. She lived for her students. Every day of this life. This life, almost over.

"That's better," said Sanjay. "Deep breaths. And blow out, like blowing out birthday candles."

She looked down at her hand, tight in a fist. Unfolded her fingers to find the letter crumpled into a ball. She made a wish, and blew on it, and it tumbled down the stairs to the gutter.

The university continued its life. The world could not bring itself to stop spinning and throw everyone off from loss of gravity. But in the History Department, gossip spun and orbited, its faculty, administration and students not fully aware of the events that began in the last days. Neither were they aware if those events involved only one great man, or were a product of the university society, or, as was usually suspected, if history itself was somehow to blame. But as the sun warmed the corners of Coleridge Park, most in that frozen city were glad to sit and soak up the sunlight filtering through their respective windows.

Dmitri sat on his office love seat and stared at the glass of vodka on top of Anna's letter. The liquid was amber in the sun, and shimmered as Dmitri bumped the side table. He wanted to call Anna, but from where he sat he found it impossible to reach his phone. He'd supported the Dean's decision, even though he found it difficult to say out loud. Anna's work had taken a downward trajectory (his phrase, and proud of the way it cushioned any blows), and her behaviour over the last half year could at best be described as erratic. He was as concerned about how she might behave now, with a copy of the letter in her hand. When he could reach the phone, if it happened today, he would caution her to not burn bridges, or act impulsively, or blame everyone else. Better that she imagined other pursuits. The terrible truth was that no one wanted to hear about the birth of romance. No student would get a better job because of it. He sighed, and reached for his glass. Half of it lined his throat. These were not romantic times.

Christophe sat outside his front door, fresh from one of his final ski trips in Mont Royal park. The sun painted golden everything that was normally grey and brown. He couldn't bring himself to get up and open the door to go inside. He was tired, yes, but energized too. His skiing obliterated the memories of the hateful Chair and

Dean for at least an hour, and were replaced by the gleeful memory of exposing Anna's romance novel. Now he would be there for her, and she would see how the rest of the faculty was deluded. A saviour in tights and tuque. The gesture, despite its initial pain, would turn out to be the most romantic.

The Dean sat in a sun dappled restaurant in a corner booth, finishing a late lunch with the university's top brass, including the Chancellor. She did not want it to end at this moment, and so stretched out the story she'd begun about how she'd saved the reputation of her department, and the university, and perhaps the city. She believed she painted the colours of her triumph in golden hues, flecked with the garnish that she had also saved the university truckloads of money by sidestepping another tenured prof. It was only History. The brass laughed, ironically. The sunlight on her skin and hair made her look…well, if not romantic, at least it softened a few edges.

Former Professor Anna Eden Hill sat by the window of her turret and stared at nothing.

"Oh it's not that bad Anna," said Dotty. "You've got to get out and do things. Instead of sitting in your house all the time. What about that Frenchman?"

"Haven't heard from him."

"Or that nice neighbour?"

"Deserted me and the renovations. I never see him."

Dotty sighed. "Just get some fresh air then." Dotty was a great believer in fresh air. "We'll see you soon anyway. Tomorrow."

Anna had no plans to go back to the suburbs, but she said see you soon too, and then almost by instinct, or more likely by ingrained obedience, she took off her sweatpants and put on real clothes and walked down the quiet streets. She did feel better. She noticed the sun was out. Anna kept walking. Her toes didn't get cold, not as soon. In half an hour she noticed she was halfway down the road to La Falaise and her Aunt Pearl. She wasn't exactly at the right point in her life to go cheer up her aunt, but at the least the two could commiserate and stare out windows together. She could finally meet the mystery woman, maybe push her chair to the windows to feel the sun. When Anna arrived at the front desk a woman made a quick call, her voice low, her eyes checking on Anna. If she could wait a minute, please. Anna said she didn't want to be any trouble.

"Oh, no trouble at all."

The director appeared, and took Anna into a small office. "I'm afraid there's no easy way to say this," she said, easily. "Your aunt died last week."

Anna crunched her forehead. "Last week? No, I talked to my mother today. You mean someone else."

The director arranged pens on her desk. "Well the thing is. The thing is your mother knew. She asked that we keep it quiet. Because of your. Because of your…situation. She said you had some personal affairs to take care of."

Anna started to say something, but found that once again she couldn't breathe. Her mouth was open and into it dripped a steady stream of salty tears. She had no idea she was crying. She didn't even know her aunt. She didn't care.

"Deep breaths," the director said.

"Where is she?" Anna sniffled. "My aunt."

"At the funeral home, I'd expect. The funeral is tomorrow."

"Tomorrow?" Anna forgot about not breathing. "You were going to tell me this when?"

"You'll have to talk to your mother about that. She said you and your aunt weren't that close."

"Closer than most," Anna said.

"Your husband—or who I thought was your husband, apparently he's your ex-husband—was with her in these last weeks. She was transformed. Lived every day as if it were her last."

"Good timing, at least." Anna wiped her tears with the tissues on the desk.

"We encourage mobility. Appropriate risks. Otherwise seniors can experience low self-esteem, feelings of hopelessness."

Anna pressed her fingers to her eyes, hard.

"She wanted to do so many things. That's how she died. She was helping outside…"

"Outside?"

"We always support independence, to avoid depression and isolation. Your aunt formed new friendships."

"With Zap?" What the hell had he wanted from her. There was no money.

"He wasn't there, unfortunately. He would have loved it. But she was out there, shoveling snow like a trooper…"

"Shoveling snow? In a wheelchair?"

"She did fine on her plastic leg. There were handrails."

22. Ghastly, Unexpected Ends

Anna wondered if there should be dancing at funerals. A huge symbolic prosthetic leg at the front of the church, to replace the god nailed down who couldn't move. At *her* funeral, white lilies would line the walls and pillars. Mourners and lovers and every student whose lives she touched would fill the pews, dance to the chorus of angels in the cheap seats. Singing the joy she brought to hearts, proclaiming the example she set for women everywhere by rising up from certain defeat.

Her funeral wouldn't look like this. Twelve people, including the priest and his apprentice or whatever they were called.

This would normally be the time to reflect. To assess what was important, judge her behaviour. She put off seeing her aunt, and now looked what happened: closed casket. Didn't even get face to face. But she wasn't in the mood for grand realizations, or taking stock, or marvelling at the frailty of this precious life.

Anna sat on a bench behind her lying mother, and kept her head down as if deep in prayer and mourning. Perhaps she did pray. But not for departed souls.

What she wanted was simple. To use this church for its true purpose. Marriage. To fulfill that vow, taken months ago while dressed in the habit of a virgin bride. What she wanted had not changed. Her near misses only made it stronger. Romance was still an empty chamber in her heart. She made the sign of the cross.

She wasn't old-fashioned. She didn't believe marriage would save her. Nobody got married in Quebec anymore. Or entered a church. And nobody was happier, or sadder, or more pregnant, or less faithful. But she could see herself skipping down this aisle, a crown of flowers in her hair, Christophe at the altar, sober and gorgeous and passionate. He would take her in his arms. She would have found someone to love, and someone that loved her. The bells would peal.

She remembered her cell phone was on, fished in her purse and turned it to mute.

The bells would peal, and they would share their lives. That was all she expected out of marriage. That and to be held. And that only sometimes.

She took advantage of her position to pray for her job back. Specifically she prayed that Dmitri and the Dean would meet ghastly, unexpected ends this weekend. In the wilds of the Laurentians, or in the glacial waters of the Saint Lawrence Seaway. Or even in the supposed safety of their corner offices. Their decision would be forgotten in the outpouring of sorrow. For her part of the bargain she promised to come to their funerals. She might dance.

In front of her, people rose and sat, chanted and sang, prayed and wept. Anna stayed where she was. She warmed up to this. Piety felt good. She might pick up this religion thing. She put a curse on Zap, who couldn't find it in his spirit to finish her turret, and hadn't showed up for his new best friend's funeral. She wasn't sure if curses were part of this church's program, but religion was a personal thing. Anna cursed the roof of Zap's house. She prayed that it would leak, and that the leak couldn't be found, and that the paint on the walls would form bulbous wet blisters of damage. Then she quickly took that back, since it was so close to her house, and she didn't want any jinx spillage. She prayed for patience instead. Beside her, late mourners filed into her pew, but she kept her focus and her closed eyes. She already felt more patient. People stood and sat, stood and sat. Someone put their hand on her shoulder. She slapped it off.

"*Putain.*"

Christophe sat down. He shook himself like a wild thing.

───※───

"Maybe they had a point," he whispered.

Anna looked at him.

"You do have to admit, you have accused everyone else of causing your problems, but not yourself. You accuse even me."

Dotty turned and shushed Anna.

"It wasn't me talking," she said. She pointed at Christophe. Dotty smiled at Christophe. He put his hand on her shoulder, and she turned back. Then he put the same hand on Anna's hand, and placed it on his leg, and slowly moved it up.

"You know you're the only one for me," he said.

Anna yanked her hand away. Do that again, and I'll leave you. She thought.

He took her hand back in his. Anna stood up and was ready to storm out of the church on her own. Halfway down the side alley she realized she pulled Christophe along. She stopped behind a pillar.

"You're upset," Christophe said, "and of course you should be. They have been hard on you." He didn't let go of her hand.

"What have I been doing all these years?"

"You should not have gone into History. Not just anyone can do it."

"Lord have mercy upon us," the priest said.

"Christ, have mercy upon us," the people said.

"You really think so?" said Anna.

"No one else is on your side. Not even your mother, hiding things from you. They're all lying to you. I have the truth."

"And what is your truth?" The church was silent as everyone bowed to pray.

"The truth is, I have cancelled my project, *la Grande McGill*. They do not deserve it. I did it for you."

"What?"

Everyone in the church turned towards the pillar they now stood in front of. The priest cleared his throat. Anna crossed herself, just in case. "What do you mean for me? she whispered.

"In solidarity."

"I just now told you they denied my tenure."

"Of course. I saw it coming."

She leaned back against the cold pillar. All he had to do now was kiss her. She would understand everything.

That kiss might have happened too, amid death and candles and prosthetic legs, had it not been for the voice of one crying in the wilderness.

"Oh death," he began, "where is your Spitfire?"

At the back of the church, alone on the balcony.

"Great leader of the Ferry Command!"

The meagre audience turned in shock. Zap stood with his arms spread, wearing a top hat and a robe normally reserved for the choir.

"Is he drunk?" Christophe asked Anna. "Or is he just an egomaniac?"

"We are not finished the service," the priest said. Zap didn't notice.

"Were you a fighter pilot, as you claimed? Or did you fight off pilots?"

"Isn't that your friend?" Dotty said to Anna.

"Did you deliver Spitfires, or you did you spit fire yourself? Did they spin you on the Gravity Machine, oh grey angel; did the Mosquito bite you, did you love men you weren't supposed to love, flight instructors, commandos?"

Most of the mourners thought the service had taken a turn for the better. At least three of them had got to know Zap at La Falaise, and had also been moved by his advocacy for the enjoyment of life. At this age, their minds were open to a more malleable belief in what constituted a funeral. So successful was Zap's tribute that one gentleman, who claimed to be a close student of history and aviation, startled the others by proclaiming that he too could fly, and would soon join Zap on the balcony to prove his belief.

"You were a spy, a spy in the house of the unloved," preached Zap, "you lost one leg in the war against age, and a breast too, and then they took your memories."

The priest sent his acolyte up to the otherwise empty balcony. But the director of La Falaise stood and said she would take care of it.

"People are asked to talk about the deceased after the ceremony," the priest suggested.

"Killer!" Anna shouted.

Zap leaned over the balcony. "I want people to live," he said. "You should be so lucky."

"You're a liar and you're a thief," she said.

"Let it all out," he said. He doffed his top hat to her.

Two mourners left. That made five still in the pews.

Christophe stayed silent. He let go of Anna's hand.

"I would like to say a few words," Zap said.

"Don't you know respect," Anna said.

"Pearl said she loved you," he said. "She said she respected you. I respect you."

"Give the girl a break," Christophe said. "She was just denied tenure."

"Oh thank you," Anna said. "Would you like a microphone?"

"It's just five people and a priest," Christophe said. "They hardly count."

"Hey," said Zap. "Pearl said she was a pilot in the war. But she didn't want to do it. You can be talented at something you don't want to do."

"I'm not sure that was entirely true," said the director, who now stood beside Zap in the balcony.

"You see?" said Anna. "You're making up these stories. You have no shame."

"Respect," he said, "is not about keeping your voice down. Respect is raising your voice. Respect proclaims the dead."

Dotty beamed. "Hello Mr. Zap," she said. She waved.

"Don't let the world be you coffin, Anna Hill."

"Get off that balcony," Anna said. "Get out of my life."

"I am your life. I am the way. The truth, the light."

The priest shook his head, crossed himself.

"I am also the death of you. I am the lost, the lie, the dark."

The priest now prayed, fervently.

"Never come to my house again," Anna said. "Or I will call the police. I will call the police now."

Christophe pulled at her hand. He dragged her to the doors.

The director appeared on the stairs. She guided Zap to the doors too, and kept Anna from him.

"You ruin everything," Anna said.

"Not true," he said. "I saved your turret."

"*Connard*," Christophe said, but kept Anna in front of him.

The last mourners watched as they went through the doors. A kind of peace descended on the church. Dotty motioned for the priest to hurry up and finish.

Outside the church, Zap was finally quiet. But Anna still howled at him, the root of all her problems. Christophe tried to let go of her hand and back away, but she didn't let him. She pulled him closer, though he cringed the closer he got to Zap. The director stood in front of Zap and tried to make peace. She said, "You know, Mr. Zap was a comfort to Pearl."

"He's a con man."

"You're smart," Zap said. "You're an amazing researcher. But I know your secret. You want to create, too. I read it you know. I saw myself there."

Anna lunged at him, and Christophe reluctantly stumbled behind her. But the director was large and not easily moved.

"I will leave," Zap said. "Your turret just needs a little paint now. You could do it yourself. You could do everything yourself. You could live your life yourself."

Zap looked at her. Anna had never seen his eyes so soft.

"Pearl," the director said, "she took appropriate risks. He didn't kill her. He freed her."

Christophe rolled his eyes.

"I'm going away, you won't see me for a long time. I'm going to build a castle too," Zap said. "They need help with their turrets."

"You see," Christophe said.

"I hope your nun finds what she's looking for. In that arid desert."

At the mention of her romance novel, Zap ripped back a veil of night to reveal her private sun, everything she thought hers and protected. She prepared to turn into to dust. But instead she stood alive and alone. She hoped her eyes appeared soft too. Anna turned and walked away and didn't look back.

Christophe glared at Zap, and followed her. Jackson Zaporzan watched with the director, and grinned. He bowed, and swept his top hat in front of him. The director dropped a coin inside.

⁓⁓

He held Sunlight in his hands. Sanjay's smile was rigid. He said, "I have finished my story," and set the bottle in her hands.

"Thank you, Sanjay."

"I mean, I have thrown it away." He looked behind him. "I gave up the script of my romantic comedy. I wished Ms. V. to play the lead. She is beautiful but cannot act her way out of a samosa. My wife is relieved. But I finally had my writing quoted. In a book on how to write. In the chapter on over-use of beautiful adjectives."

"I'm happy."

"You say you are happy, but you are sad. Mr. Zap has moved out. He came to say goodbye too. He apologized that he rented the house to a fraternity."

"I rented mine to Audrey."

Sanjay nodded. He glanced at the two houses and grimaced.

Christophe had to do nothing to convince Anna. After the funeral he said, "Let's get out of here." And Anna instantly knew what he meant. She was almost one hundred percent sure she knew what he meant. She asked just in case.

"To Paris?"

He looked at her for a few moments with those dark eyes. "Of course to Paris." He smiled broadly. She realized she'd rarely seen him like that. Almost exposed. She didn't mention marriage. He'd probably crumble in a pile of vulnerability.

They ran to her house. Anna laughed and swore. He said he wanted to calm her down and brought her to her bedroom, and he petted her naked back for almost a minute before he flipped her over. He laughed too, and swore in imitation of her, and when he entered her his eyes scared her almost more than his hands around her neck.

The invitation to Paris wasn't like she imagined it. But then she'd imagined a lot of things, hadn't she. And everything else back here was dead.

Anna kept imagining. She thought meeting with Dmitri would be awkward and cold. He'd offered her the "terminal year" contract to stay and wrap things up in the next year, but just the sound of the contract made her uncomfortable. Dmitri tried to make her comfortable, but without shifting blame. If she wanted to appeal, she could. Or they could try and spin the romance novel. Anna squinted at him, trying to see where he'd heard about that, but was too afraid to ask.

"The romance novel," he said, "could be an ironic twist on gender commentary. That gender says how we should be, not how we are. Look at Diane Silverbow."

He pointed to a picture on his desk. Yes, they were seeing each other.

"But her name is not Silverbow. She is Diane Silverstein. And I am not convinced about the Diane part. She was fulfilling how she thought she should be. And me too. Dressed as Napoleon every year."

"You're a good exile," Anna said.

"But if you stay for Terminal, you'll see my new costume. Next year at History Faculty Welcomes, I will come as Chief the Crazy Horse."

"Or the Sitting Bull," Anna said.

But no, she wouldn't stay for the terminal year. A year of shame and winter, versus a new spring and exotic romance in Paris. If she didn't leave with Christophe, she'd end up living in her mom's sewing room upstairs. Assisted living.

So they gave her classes to Audrey. She'd already said 'contract adjunct' was the new tenure. But Audrey was a foreign country.

Anna left Dmitri's office without tears.

In the morning Anna, ill-slept, stood dressed at the bedroom door and listened to the self-satisfied snorts of her destiny and told him in a voice softer than snow that they would leave for their Paris. In the first days of spring or forever, mercy me.

23. The Queen of Coleridge Park

With stubborn joy Anna flung open the shutters and beamed into the golden thread of Paris streets. Her tangle of rosy hair hid her nakedness and flapped from the window like a bride's bed sheets. She was no longer a predictable girl from the suburbs, she was Queen of Heaven, she was Satan's masterpiece, she was the Form of Light.

She stood on her toes and watched her stained white shirt float from the window to the river below. The Seine caught it and carried it away, detoured it around Notre Dame. The shirt could fly, but Anna was grounded. Done with flight. She would linger forever in this bedroom with the windows open to splendour, despite the chill, despite the sudden replacement of sun with cloud. Rochester the cat perched on the sill, satisfied as Anna was to watch the world glide by the window.

This morning like no other, in a tasteful fortress on the Seine.

She and Christophe ran from spite and gossip. An academic Bonnie and Clyde. Brigitte and Serge. Two cells as one, the burden of isolation lifted with sunrise. They could not stop the laughter inflight while they traded stories of their employers and students and indiscretions, and breezed through the curiosity of customs with a medicated cat. She felt the power of last night's wine in her veins. They landed, they drank, he told her to tie up her hair, she was in France now. In the next seconds she spilled wine on her shirt. Tomorrow she—they— would shop at Printemps for a month's wardrobe if need be.

Like no other, of delicious uncertainty.

"We can close this window?" Christophe through layers of pillow and Pomerel. She turned, gazed upon his form, his body free from the sheets, golden too. His arm draped over his eyes, his sex tumescent in morning glory.

"Off with my overcoat, off with my gloves," Anna sang, "who needs an overcoat, I'm burning with love."

"*Je dois aller pisser.*"

She straddled him.

Last night he passed out. The jet lag, the red-eye, the red wine. She watched him sleep, listened to the bass rumble of his breath. Anna was the downfall of all men, none could resist; but this would have to wait. She delayed her attack on the castle of love till dawn.

Now she slid on top of him and wondered, how would her nun scale his walls? How would she make him love her?

1. Thesis: Every (medieval) history student knows of *The Dove's Neck-Ring*, of Ibn Hazm. The fire that is latent in flint remains hidden—unless friction occurs.

2. Thesis: A lack of love can be supplemented with a love potion administered daily among high-risk subjects. A modern-day medical miracle. A dash of testosterone and estrogen for the first weeks; an ounce each of pheromones and dopamine for the thrill; topped up with oxytocin for that long-lasting flavour. And three tines of wild rose thorns.

Christophe rubbed his temples. The potion had lingering side effects. May cause dizziness, loss of self, changes in patterns and rhythms of speech, lack of appetite, confusion about identity, place and time, false or unusual sense of well-being, pain, fear, death. Anna stopped the friction. She took Christophe's hands and pinned them behind his head.

"I must go." He lifted her off, a dove to him, feather and hollow bone. She watched him move across the room. The room was his, Paris was his, her body. He stretched and she imagined a wild cat. He walked through the doorway a lion and when he came back she would tame him. Not a young thing anymore, but more attractive because of it. Waited for others to make the kill. A steady pace, all the strength in the shoulders, blinking, as if he last ate three days ago and is still unconcerned with dinner. He needs nothing. He doesn't even need her. Not like she needs him. Anna sits on the edge of the bed. She would offer her neck to this lion of Paris. Because he didn't need her.

And all she asked in return was herself, and his universe.

Christophe came back, pants on, held a fresh white shirt. The conference was starting, no more time. He wasn't happy to leave, he said, but they wanted him to speak so much they were even willing to pay.

"They got you in there quickly," Anna said.

"Connections," he said.

She ran her hand down his breastbone while he buttoned between the fingers.

"I'm staying," she said. "Rochester and me."

"Of course."

"No more conferences."

"Ever again. They're not for you."

"Get out of here. My love." She kissed him, any open skin. "I need you to leave."

The corners of his mouth twitched.

She pushed him away and closed the linen curtains. The sun played no more across his chest. She would chain herself to his desk. She would be free. She would complete her romance within these walls, unencumbered and open, free to create and explore. Someday she would go back to Montreal, collect her things, sell her house. But not now. Neither during the summer. The sounds of this tiny Parisian isle, the clatter of tourists and boats, the smells of diesel and urban river. The dust would settle. And clothes—she would no longer wear clothes. The costume she wore was the last she needed.

Christophe laughed. "You are only in love."

He understood her. They were the same. They were unlike anyone else.

We rode through the uncharted forests of Iberia, avoiding thieves and villages and wolves. We cut through thick forests and mosquito-filled marshes, forded rivers and drank brackish water. This was as far as I'd travelled from my home and abbey. I'd never gone more than a day's journey, and that was by foot. We saw no inns. The Moor kept us away from people. I could tell from the way his brow furrowed when he saw strangers in the distance that he had no love for them, whatever their belief. His hand went more readily to his belt and daggers when we saw people than when we saw beasts. He smelled them before he saw them. His broad nose up, his eyes dark. He muttered unintelligible language. But when he smelled the red deer he lay still in the dirt. His skin dark and his ivory robes, the red ochre of his sash, the coarseness of his wiry beard on my alabaster skin. The sun of Al-Andalus, the warmth of his devotion to animals was like his devotion to me. He lifted the horse's hooves one by one with barely a tickle on their fetlocks, checking for rot and wear. He hobbled the horse by tying the legs together. The horse was black like the Moor, and free as I felt. Tiny steps would never take it far. Occasionally he would give the horse a day off, and the two of us would walk leagues beside it. I grew to love the animal as I grew to love the Moor. He was a silly thing, scared of quick rabbits but happy to squash snakes underfoot. But like the Moor he had no fear of travel. I had heard the stories of the Moors and Arabs, of their migrations, their trade over the seas, the annual pagan pilgrimage to the Ka'aba in Mecca. Both of these beasts, man and horse, had undoubtedly seen the world.

And yet, I was seized by a terrifying doubt: where in that world was he taking me? The romance we discovered, did he truly feel it? Why would he take me so many days' journey from my land?

That night by the waters he spread the patterned carpets under the watchful eyes of unseen beasts, hidden from hounds and hunters.

With murderous glances, languishing; their eyelids are sheaths for glances like swords.

I, Harmonía, let down my plaited locks then, and mourned that I should sleep, and die, and not see my love tomorrow.

I lay in his arms and burned in the fire of passion, offered the final solace, and it left me in ashes; and it left me the core of who I was. But when I took back all who I was through the Moor, he lay on his carpets on the sand an ordinary man.

Anna believed the air of Paris was to blame for the changes in her writing. How had her Moor become ordinary? Nobody wanted to read about an ordinary man. And hadn't she killed the horse back at the abbey? And when had Angeles renamed herself Harmonía?

One day we came closer to a village than I had seen for days, desperate for food and water. I knew the danger. Men killed a stranger sooner than ask questions. Unchecked, strangers made their way into sheltered places and sowed havoc and sorrow. They questioned and bred strange habits. Pilgrims from other worlds, heading towards Santiago or farther. To the site of miracles. Like the site of our own miracle. Someday, not far away, the world would discover the place we, the nun and Moor, invented romance, and they would build a shrine filled with relics—his dagger, my torn cloaks, the fringe of his red sash—and pilgrims would flock to the holy sands. But for now we lovers were hunted, for now we were feared. A devil and his familiar.

He devised a tent for me, on top of the horse. I would be covered completely, my pink skin shielded from the restless gazes of men. A Moor leading a Christian woman might be excuse enough for a battle. And no one even with the hint that I was a nun. Was once a nun. That now I am

a woman, slender, lissome, of fresh beauty, filling the caravan with fragrance of herself. By her is every desert peopled, and by her is every mirage transformed to abundant water.

He was drawn to water all the time. Whenever he found some he dismounted and performed his ablutions. After love if there was no water near (I could tell he was in the mood when he began to search for streams) he would use some of our precious drinking water. In the canyons I revealed the rose-shaped bruise on my thigh, and he showed me how to bathe.

He scooped up the water and began with his mouth. His lips glistened with sweat and me and he rinsed them off. He rinsed his nose and all he could smell. He stood naked by the river and poured water over his head three times, over his right shoulder, over his left shoulder. His hands to the wrists. He shook the dust of roads and kingdoms from his feet.

The Moor took my hand and motioned for me to wash my mouth. The water was clear and fresh. It hung on my lips. I licked them. I followed his pantomimes for the rest. My fine nose, my thin fingers, shoulders, between my legs. He poured water over my wheat-coloured hair and I shivered. Right shoulder, left shoulder. He took each foot in his hands and with caresses made them clean. In his deep voice he intoned prayers or wishes. I laughed when he toweled me dry, left me standing on a rock by the waters. From the baggage on his horse he produced a leather satchel, small but heavy. It made metallic noises. He set it down in front of me. He undid the rope and reached in, and pulled out an armlet set with rubies, and bracelets, this one silver, the other gold. He slid them high on my wrists. On my fingers rings of sapphire, around my neck a silver pendant shaped like a crescent moon, filled with cloth soaked in perfumes. Last, a pair of intricate gold earrings set with glazed quartz. But my ears were not pierced, so the Moor did it right there with a needle. I didn't move until the earrings hung from my sensitive lobes. Then the Moor produced a pot of oil, and his strong hands and fingers covered every part of my body with it until I shone in the waning light. And then I wanted a mirror, something I had not seen since I was young, and so bent over the river and watched my fragmented finery. As I bent I reached out to the Moor to steady myself, and he took my hand, and the other, and he bound them together behind my back with a soft cord.

I laughed at him again. But he didn't laugh. He withdrew from his baggage another package, and pulled out a white cotton haik and wrapped it around me. Then he lifted me to the top of the horse and fastened the tent over me. That was the last time I saw him alive.

"You are what?"

"In Paris. I'm not sending you my book. I can bring it to you in person."

"For how long?"

"I may stay here the rest of my life."

"Wonderful. You finally gave birth."

"No, I…"

"Birth of Romance. With your professor? Have a pancake for me. So, what did the Moor do?"

"He kidnapped her. He'll sell her into slavery."

Silence. More of that.

"So you gave up the university."

"It was mutual."

"For writing. For the money and glory."

"For now."

"Good girl. Okay, history. First Romance Novel. *The Sheik*. 1919. You with me? Still in print. Kidnapped and raped by the Sheik, heroine suffers violent treatment so falls in love with her tormentor. Another Sheik kidnaps her away. Sheik One gets her back—he's wounded, what. Realizes he loves her so: sends her away. She grabs a pistol, uh-huh, tries to kiss herself goodbye, Sheik stops her and never lets her go, end."

Silence from Anna this time.

"So," Julia said.

"So."

"It can't be the last time she sees him."

"No it can't."

"You've got a rolling start to the romance. Now how does it end. You've got to write *to* the end. For the end. We all end. And romances set in the Medieval thingy, they end with the *mujer* second banana to the *hombre*. Who above all, fortunately, wants to fulfill her wishes. Call me when you're done."

"Mu-jair?"

"Mu-hair. However you say it, it's woman."

> I knew my fate. I had heard it whispered back at the abbey, the stories of my childhood, of whole villages of women abducted by pirates. Caravans crossing a vast desert, horrid barbarities visited on Christian ladies. One nun nothing.
>
> The Moors didn't seek men to harvest their coffee and pluck the rose of saffron. They wanted to fill their concubines. Evil, evil women. It was to prevent the spread of immorality, they said. To satiate the sexual desires of the female slaves. They had no idea of woman's yearning.
>
> From my tent I heard the clatter of the town. Rising voices in the language of the Moor, dogs barking, horses' hooves, tiny bells and the call to prayer. Chickens scattering in front of me, the hammer of the blacksmith, the crack of his fire. Carts and distant music. The waters of fountains. Coins counted. The labyrinth of the souk. I would be sold.
>
> Yet the horse continued, wound down the cobblestones until the noise quieted, until only the calls of women and laughter of children reached my ears. I tried to move the haik to see. One

eye was free, but the tent still obstructed my view. Now I saw shadows, shadows through a mist of tears. When we stopped I heard the Moor's voice. Someone else held the horse. Someone touched my leg. A small hand. A boy.

I kicked at him, and he laughed. His hand explored further up my leg. When he got to my knee a woman called out what sounded like an admonishment. Her voice nearer, until the boy either left or stood away from the horse. I shouted to her. I shouted for help. I knew the Arabic word. In Spanish I pled my cause and asked for the mercy of woman on woman.

"He will sell me for a trinket," I said. "He will brand me with hot irons. I who was once a Bride of Christ have become the chattel of a beast, my vows shattered, doomed for eternity. He who promised everything has left me with nothing. I pray for some drowsy syrups from your household, enough to release me from this sin and let me be with my Husband in the next world."

I never knew who the woman was, and whether she had pity because she was Christian or knew of nuns or only of the suffering of women. But she did speak my language, for some minutes later hands came underneath her tent, and found my bound hands. Into them she put a small vial. All was quiet.

Seconds later the Moor took off the tent and pulled me off the horse so quickly I almost dropped the philter. We went through the arched door into a courtyard, and before a wide and bearded man and a metal table of mint tea and dates he stripped off my cloak so I stood naked but for my pearls and sapphires. He untied my wrists and rubbed them free of marks, but did not look inside my fists. When he turned me around in front of the man I quickly brought the vial to my nose, looked at it, smelled it. As an infirmaress I had tended the abbey herb garden, had mixed the potions and memorized my star charts. I knew my humours and their seasons, the holes to cut in skulls to release spirits. But all my learning could not penetrate the bottle. I needed to taste and smell it to know its effects. The murky green meant lettuce certainly, with purple mulberry juice. Also necessary were opium and hemlock. If I were lucky, bryony for hallucination. I only needed too much.

The fat man asked to see my buttocks. He said they reminded him of the dunes of his great deserts, between them the oasis of the Ubari. When the men both stared as I bent over the table, I gave each mint tea a dose from the vial. I stood apart from them now. They reclined on their cushions and sipped their tea with greed and lust. I lowered my eyes and remembered my home and let a smile play on my lips. The fat man and Moor laughed at my coyness, and money changed hands.

Moments later, the coins fell from their hands and onto the tiled floors, some of it rolling to my feet. I bent and picked them up, bit into one or two. The men were sprawled now on their cushions, the whites of their eyes showing, their mouths silent. The fat one took longer. I stripped the Moor of all his vestments, of his headscarves and robes and sandals, and put them on. I stripped the other man too, and bundled up his clothes and put them in the Moor's bag. All the dates. All the coins. Then I strode out the door and leapt onto the Moor's horse, pushing away the boy who held it, and galloped 'til I could see no more the minarets.

The End

"Right. Happily, ever after."
"She took over. I had nothing to do with it, Julia."
"Heard of that. Never believed it."

"I'm thinking it's not quite the end. She goes back to lead the *Reconquista* and drive the Moors from Spain."

"Your readers want your heroine to kill her lover and join the army. You've given this some thought."

She had. And she hadn't.

"Send me the manuscript. Now get out."

She'd finished the ending by the second day of the conference, Christophe at the Sorbonne with another talk, or a panel—she didn't want to know. When she hung up the phone the room on the Seine was quiet. Did she want to give it more thought? She'd got the story down. Intrigue and betrayal, love and loss. All the trappings of a heartbreaking, exotic kidnapping. Some things had to be left alone. Sometimes magic needed more space than logic. She'd left the university so she could stop analysing everything.

But she deserved a crepe. She put on boots, boots with heels. She shouldered her satchel, empty of page. At the first stand she requested one with lemon and sugar. Simple. Her arrival was complete. She ate the ambrosia while she watched the ghosts of French peasants forever marching to the Crusade of the Faint-Hearted.

She walked to the Petit Pont, thought she might pick up a book or two—a novel, nothing academic. The lemon bit at her lips. At Shakespeare & Company she knew she was just blocks from the Sorbonne, and smiled. Her arrival wasn't complete after all. All she needed was to have one more crepe standing beside the Seine. With Nutella this time, so that the chocolate melted among buttery folds and painted her fingers. And shared with Christophe. She hurried to rescue him.

Outside conference room doors she heard the familiar tones, the languages of science and art uncomfortably wed. If she were French she could walk into the room, pout, stride out. And he would run after her, and she would tell him Julia wanted to see her manuscript. Or was that an American movie ending. But she couldn't even bring herself to open the door. What if he didn't know the script?

But that was silly, wasn't it, and what had she quit the university for, if not to free herself from constraint.

She opened the door and its creaks made everybody turn to her. She forgot to look at faces. The small room looked like a corner of Versailles, with tall windows and ornate chandeliers, painted niches and mirrors, conference tables lining the walls. Someone motioned for her to close the door. She scanned faces, found none familiar, and closed it with a bang.

After a few more dead ends, she found an official looking table. They couldn't find his name on the conference time table, but Anna explained he'd only come on at the last minute. They directed her to an organizer who knew Christophe's name. He claimed they hadn't invited him, but he had seen him in the halls. Asking about positions, looking for work, it seemed. Asking everywhere. Last saw him at the *Librarie Philosophique*, asking them.

Anna said, I mean Professeur Christophe Auguste de Latour de Mantes-La-Jolie. That Christophe.

The organizer smirked. That Christophe.

"Why do you have that little smile," Anna said. "What's that mean? Why does 'That Christophe' get a little smile?"

He puffed out his cheeks and blew.

Anna pushed his chest.

"No blowing," she said. "No little smiles and no blowing. Got that?"

"Madame," he said.

"And none of that either."

Down the hall from an open room there was laughter. Anna looked to see if more French were making fun of her. She could feel her heart beat, too fast. She would not analyse why the man was so awful. He was French. One got frustrated with the French, that was all. When she turned back the man had escaped.

Anna sat on a bench. She puffed out her cheeks and blew. It felt good, so she did it a few more times. It felt much better than thinking about Christophe lying to her about speaking here, on the first days in these Elysian Fields. But in the next minute, as if she had willed him to life, he walked in front of her. His head down, muttering to himself, his briefcase a weapon to frighten students.

"Christophe!"

"Ah, Anna."

"What are you doing?"

"Yes, going to give another talk. A little busy, can we talk later?"

She stood up and grabbed his sleeve. She blew air from her cheeks once more. Why could her nun do it, and not she? Bound and shackled. When he shook off her grip and looked around him, she spoke in the kind of voice she usually reserved for saying goodbye to dying cats.

"You don't have to lie to me anymore," she said. "This is us, in Paris."

His eyes were wide. He shook his head and put his hand on her shoulder. "I am late. But listen to me, you are my truth. I never lie to you."

He pointed down the hall. Students and professors grouped around a door as if going to a lecture. "You see?"

Anna nodded. Maybe it was the air of Paris, saturated with diesel and history. She blew away that smog, and thought she saw the outline of an ordinary man. "Okay. I'm coming to listen then. I wanted a crepe, on the Seine."

"You don't want more conferences anymore. That's not for you. Classes and lectures and history. You're not an academic, not now, not ever. Go to our home, to your fables and romance."

He already rushed down the hall, jostled into the crowd. At the end of the corridor she thought she saw him stop in front of someone, bring his hands together in a plea.

Anna walked behind, bumping into people she hardly saw. Her vision clouded, her face hot. She reached up and undid her hair, let it spill out of control on her shoulders. Around the door, normally dour profs and serious students laughed at something. Her first instinct was to pull her hair back up, wipe her cheeks. But she saw they were enthralled by someone at a table.

"Your cornices are critical," he said, "your slate tiles have slipped." He put his arm around the timid man who stood beside him, who wore a tunic and held a crude mallet. "I offered to help. Like you can see, I got lots of experience with turrets."

The table advertised that medieval castle being built from scratch in the Burgundy woods. The same re-creation Christophe had mocked as populist the first time they'd been at the conference, the tunic-sporting, time-traveling academic he'd shunned. Now the man beamed at the carpenter next to him. "So anyway, there was the Queen of Coleridge Park," he said, "hanging from the tower by one hand, a book in the other." His voice a mix of French and *Québécois* accents. "Her hair a rose blossom on an ivy wall, but huge flakes of snow on her neck bit with a thousand frozen teeth. 'I refuse to get hypothermia in my own castle,' she said. The pigeons on the next window leapt into the air and made little snowstorms of their own."

He let his audience soak up the exotic image for a few moments, let his gaze wander across the crowd until he stopped on one person. He smiled, and Anna thought instead of running down the corridors of the Sorbonne, or going back to the apartment on the Seine, or ever pretending to believe the lies of Christophe again, she would stay to hear how the story turned out.

"The book tore at the spine, and she watched her reputation tear all the way down the side of the page. And then it was free."

"*The FalconMoor*," Anna said, "a deconstruction of the parameters of romance."

"Lot of work," said Zap, "for one book."

THE END

The author wishes to acknowledge his indebtedness to the numerous editors, pilots, architects, professors and students whose complicit or unwitting guidance helped create this organism, including Karen Stoecker, Kate Speers, Luce Lafontaine, Yseult Saint-Jacques, Suzanne Morton, Patricia Ivan, Denise Audet, Monic Robillard, Josie Teed, Lori Schubert, Maurice Mierau, Biscuit and Hugo for their loyal support, and that insatiable muse, my wife.